***

Hobo's

Revenge

Dedicated to Shawn Paul Delorey

[1989 - 2013]

AND

A salute to every US veteran that engages in
a support service, a battlefield or a warzone and
defends our freedom

***

Hobo's Revenge

By William Delorey

(c) 2016

Cover Design: J Lacy Coughlan

Copy Editor: J Lacy Coughlan

Cover Images: Bill Delorey

Special thanks always to Genie for her support and encouragement over the years

Thanks to Susan Carr for her editorial support

Thanks
Professor Luke Wallin and
Writer Michael Lee
A little piece of each of you resides
in everything I write ...

A special thanks and recognition to all my brother and sister veterans who live the sacrifice that keeps this country safe from its enemies, and saves its lands for our future generations

www.billdelorey.com

Additional Fiction by William Delorey

*** Predators ***
A Six-pack of Short Fiction
A Collection by William Delorey
Some predators are animals.
Some predators are human.
Sometimes it's hard to tell the difference.
(2015)

*** Shuffle an Impulse ***
A Novel by William Delorey
A psychological suspense and medical thriller
(2015)

*** Operation Crossbow ***

A Novel by William Delorey
Deception, murder, and treachery
An Espionage Thriller
(2015)

*** Double Cross ***
A novel by William Delorey
Medicine & Money
Drug Smuggling and Organ Theft
An Espionage Thriller
November 2020

Go to author website for more information

www.billdelorey.com

Published in the United States of America

WordWizard Publications

411 Walnut Street Suite 6317
Green Cove Springs, Florida 32043

HOBO'S REVENGE
A work of fiction

Operation Vagabond illustrates violent behavior in its characters and actions, and depicts sexual situations. Language describing scenes in this novel makes it less suitable for young ages.

www.billdelorey.com

Hobo's Revenge

- Excerpt from his acceptance speech upon his
election to Congress of the United States -

Circumstantial Justice

"Any Socratic system within which the absolute terms 'guilty' or 'not guilty' apply defies any true relationship with either 'justice' or 'innocence' as our legal scholars define it today.

Whereas a true impartial judicial system relies upon defining the circumstance that triggers an action, and allows a participant to mitigate his own behavior and the behavior of others based on factors outside our convoluted legal terminology and beyond the hard and fast logic we imagine exists in case law."

Senator Miller Winston,
Massachusetts
United States Congress

HOBO'S REVENGE

Unobstructed, the knuckles hit hard and heavy. The final punch breaks two ribs, cracks two more, and empties his lungs. Jason Marks grunts and passes out. Then the towel again, the water once more soaking his head and body.

"Tell me," the assailant growls.

Marks lifts his eyes, shakes his head a fourth time, his lips split and bloody, one eye badly bruised and swelling shut. A few unintelligible words bubble out. Sounds like 'puk yo mutha'.

Two days ago, drug smugglers ambushed a Special Forces intelligence squad operating in Panama, killed three in a fire-fight, and now hold the captain and two additional rangers in a concrete bunker. Corporal Marks sits in a chair bolted to the floor of a drug storage room and struggles against the ropes binding his arms and chest.

The smuggler boss tosses the bucket aside, pulls out a knife honed razor-sharp, grabs a fist full of hair, and opens a slit beneath his prisoner's chin. "Tell me."

Corporal Marks remains mute.

The point digs in deeper, opens the slit a bit wider. A feral grin crosses his face and the blade cuts through the carotid artery neat and clean. The man jerks the knife sideways and forward, slicing through muscle and tendon as if it were wet cotton thread. He watches the federal agent bleed out.

"Fuck you, agent man," he says, his English heavily accented. "Your brother will answer or get the same. I'll show him you first."

Some people might label the killer ugly. A poorly healed scar runs from beneath his right eye, down a cheek and across thick lips on a face that's seen better days. He strides out through the door, aims his boots down a short hallway toward another locked storage room.

The man keys the lock and pushes the heavy steel door. Hung on stout, well-oiled hinges, the door opens half-way and bumps against an obstruction then rockets back at him and breaks his nose. He staggers backward across the corridor, bounces off the wall, meets a knee between his legs, coughs, and grabs his crotch with one hand, his bleeding nose with the other. A punch he never sees coming drops him face-down on the dirt floor. Still holding his crotch and nose, the smuggler squirms onto his back and groans.

A man dressed in combat fatigues lands on the killer's chest and drives a fist into his throat, crushing the trachea and tearing the esophagus. Choking on his own blood, the body twitches a couple times, then runs out of life.

"Shudda learnt how to tie real knots, asshole. Serves ya' right, leaving me alone in a room wrapped in rope a five-year-old could untangle with one hand."

The Special Forces Captain kicks the man once, turns the body on its side, releases a flap catch and confiscates a pistol. He mutters aloud, "Gotta find Marks and Klyne, we got a mission to complete."

Cooper cocks an ear, listens. Barely discernible, a small diesel generator throbs outside the building, supplying electricity. He spins in a circle, quickly evaluating the bunker.

Concrete walls buried four or five feet below grade surround a dirt floor thirty feet long, four feet wide. Short gable walls at each end vent outside and support a ridge beam. A plywood roof slopes up and overlaps the ridge. Four additional metal doors line the right side of the corridor, six storerooms altogether. Three doors open and three closed. A small but permanent stopover facility it appears, a protective drug bunker on a smuggling route heading north.

A string of dim light bulbs hangs from the ridge and illuminates the corridor. The access hallway ends at a wooden stairway that leads up to a small landing and single exit door. No windows.

Cooper slides along the wall, the pistol leading his way. He listens carefully, then peeks into room five. He finds Corporal Marks, bled out, eyes wide open in a death stare. Cooper drops his chin and closes his eyes briefly, emotion clouding his mind momentarily. That's four lost this trip, unusual for the extremely well-trained black operations unit he leads.

He continues along the corridor, approaches the door six, listens carefully. Silence. He drops into a squat, rests his butt on the dirt floor and eases the lever down. A quarter inch, then a half. Unlocked. He slowly completes the rotation, takes a full minute. He aims the pistol through his knees and into the room at gut level then rolls back slightly and kicks the door.

Empty, no humans. A large stack of wrapped kilos, heroin or cocaine maybe, sits in the middle of the room. Three backpacks and three military issue M-16 rifles belonging to himself and his team lean against a corner. Two wireless transmitters lay in the dirt, shattered. Otherwise, an empty room.

In one smooth motion, he stands, releases the clip, sticks it in his cargo pocket, rachets the remaining shell out of its chamber, catches it in mid-air and tosses the confiscated pistol behind the stack, trusting his own weapons more than an untested enemy handgun. He removes his personal Colt from a side pocket in his pack, anchors it in his waistband, and grabs his M-16, checks its loads, sets the semi-automatic burst, nods and grins.

He exits the room, crab-crawls along the hallway, approaches door four, listens. Two low voices converse in Spanish, he pushes to his feet. Extremely patient, he lifts the brass lever a quarter inch, then a half. Unlocked. He jerks the lever up completely, kicks the door, finds two men naked to the waist and playing cards, sweating in a wet Panama heat wave.

He pulls the trigger twice, a three-shot burst enters the heart of each man faster than either one can draw a weapon. He abandons both men right where they fall, and heads for the next door, tests the lever.

Locked. No keys. He glances back at the smuggler boss he'd killed, debating the key issue, watching door six, open, its light on. The shots will have warned its occupants, if any. He counts off a ten-second delay. Nothing. He shrugs, pulls the trigger and blasts the lock on door five, slides four feet backward along the wall and squats below any upper body firing line, his M-16 ready. Silence. No response. The door remains ajar, the lock blown into pieces.

"Jake," he yells, figuring this storage room holds his sergeant or maybe he's already dead behind door six, like Marks in door two.

"Yes," a single word. Sergeant Jacoby Klyne, his guy. "I'm here, Captain."

"Step out, Jake, show me your hands." Personal safety first.

Two hands appear, empty, then a full body and a face he recognizes immediately. "Nobody else in here but me, Coop." His eyes fall on the body outside door two.

"He killed Marks. The guy's dead, let's go," Cooper says. He quickly explains his escape, the dead smuggler and his two card-playing henchmen.

Sergeant Klyne and Captain Cooper retrieve their backpacks and gather all ammunition. Klyne grabs his own M-16. Cooper unloads and smashes the third weapon against the concrete wall, tosses it behind the stack. Both men exit the room and approach the landing, climb the wooden steps and ease open the door, one inch. Klyne sticks an eye to the slot. Nothing. He pushes it open another inch, catches a slight oddity in the trees and spots a wooden shack partially hidden in the foliage. Wide, flat palm fronds layer the roof and a porch surrounds the cabin on three sides.

Klyne holds one finger straight up, points at himself, then left. Points a thumb over his shoulder at the captain, points a finger right, then three fingers up and a silent count down, one finger, two, three and kicks the door. Both men launch up and out of the dugout, spinning in opposite directions. Klyne whips around the corner and ducks behind a rain barrel.

Directly behind Klyne, the captain takes one quick step to the right and his weight trips a hidden trigger. A buried trap-grenade explodes beneath him and blows him off his feet. Rusty nails, glass shards and steel shavings rip through his boot, shredding tissue and bone.

Cooper twists at the waist, drops his weapon and falls on his back, grabs what remains of his left foot below the calf, broken and bloody. A groan escapes his lips, "Fuck me that hurt!"

Tears roll down his cheeks. He loosens his belt, slides it out, wraps it around his calf four inches above the bleeding, and pulls it as tight as possible. The bleeding nearly stops.

Klyne pops up above the rain barrel, and checks out the shack. The door leading inside sits dead center on the front wall and bangs open, spits out three armed men bringing up automatic rifles, but not quick enough. All three catch M-16 body shots dead center. Sergeant Klyne never misses at such close range. He leaves them where they lie, studies the cabin a minute, and then turns back to his squad leader.

He opens his pack and a first aid kit, injects morphine into a muscle below the knee. He removes the shrapnel, stones and glass, cleans and disinfects the damaged ankle and foot as best he can, wraps a sterile bandage around the entire bloody mess. Bright red spots dot the white cloth immediately.

"Hurts, need a new foot!" A groan follows, shock arrives, and his head flops back onto the dirt. "Leave me here, Jake. Go get some help."

"Bullshit, you'll never make it alone. It's me and you, or nothing." Klyne strips his pack of all but essentials, grabs both rifles, hoists Cooper over his right shoulder, and takes the first step north. "Glad you're a runner and not a weight lifter."

"Hang in there, Coop, we got a least three days, maybe four, to the nearest Tango command once we find the river. We'll send a chopper team in to collect Marks, wipe out any smugglers still here, burn the shack and implode that building."

Chapter One

A smudge of darkness creeps across the horizon and swallows the last streak of sunlight, plunging the forest encampment into shadow. The scent of pine pitch and wood smoke hangs in the chill. Low flames lick the rim of a rusty barrel set in a clearing amidst conifers and oaks. A few random sparks spit up and flare out in the moonless dusk.

Light chatter floats beneath the gloom and sets a brighter tone. A gleeful shriek twists up into the night and elevates the mood, chasing away the frowns and sadness. Several deep chuckles follow. A tough life sometimes for these vagabonds, each one embracing that occasional bout of wit or humor simply to survive.

One more burst of laughter peals out, another high-pitched squeal. "That's too funny, wait 'til you hear this one." Another tall tale bends the facts, spicing up tragedy. True, false, or embellished, story-telling becomes an art form less easily defined when homeless drifters share a patch of ground for a day or a week, sometimes a month or more.

As the chill deepens, each bundled body cloaks itself in a ragged blanket or a dingy old coat. The travelers snuggle closer. A grunt or a groan disturbs the quiet as one or another scoots in toward the fire and crabs about the weather.

"Shoulda left a week ago." A male voice grumbles. A fabric rustle punctuates his words as he tosses a log into the barrel then slips away and wraps himself tighter. A loner and complainer, hiding near the perimeter but still slow to abandon his companions.

"Damn cold sneaks right inside these old bones, sets up a cramp." A different male voice, another fabric rustle. "Come on over here and warm me up, Annie."

A group giggle pops out. Everyone knows what's coming.

"Screw you, Gator. Git out the magnifier and use a rag." Annie giggles again. Same request every night, same response. Annie and Gator remain pals, but not lovers. An old boar hunter and alligator trapper from southern Georgia, Gator never bathes. The average nose can smell the man a mile away, even his fingernails reek.

Chicago's not the finest place in the country to sleep outdoors during winter, and most seasonal vagabonds have long departed, seeking the southern warmth.

A few hardy misfits hang around until the last minute, confiscating the favored spots soon as the alpha dogs vacate the camp. Starlight peeks between the clouds and barely penetrates the thick evergreen canopy, reflecting a light dusting of snow that began an hour ago and then quit.

In the distance, the never-sleeping city bounces its reflection off the cloud-cover. A long mournful wail accents the rhythmic clatter of large metal wheels chugging slow but steady atop steel I-beams aimed at the old dilapidated stockyards. Rolling north on the mainline railhead, four powerful engines whistle and whine and a steel tune vibrates down from treble to bass as a mile-long caravan winds into that final bend and climbs a slight rise before aiming itself at the municipal boundaries.

Long closed now, the vacant and mostly dismantled slaughterhouse once fed a major industry and anchored the Chicago economy and its surrounding agricultural communities.

One man and his woman sit off in a separate section away from the fire, close enough to others for safety but distant enough for privacy. Eleanor McGee slips a pair of silver feathers through a piercing in each ear, a gift from her current traveling companion. She leans in and plants a thank you kiss right where it counts.

Heath bought the earrings for his sister at a Navajo roadside stand on his last journey west but changed his mind after meeting Ellie at a hobo camp in New York a few months ago. He didn't share that 'gift for his sister' information with Ellie though.

Both watch the train rumble and slow, arcing into that last graceful curve. A lone shadow tosses a backpack and drops off a boxcar, stumbles once on the icy gravel slope then catches his balance and grabs the pack, slings it over a shoulder, and trots toward the hobo camp, weaving between frosty white pines and naked oaks.

Dry leaves rustle and twigs crack, and Heath Simmons turns an ear toward the noise. Wary, testing, he stands and says, "That you Tick? Couple days late."

An answer bounces back between the trees. "Yup, it's me, tardy to the party as usual. Don't make a schedule that needs keeping anymore. Figured you'd wait or move on and I'd track you south somewhere a bit warmer."

Tick pushes through the brush, drops his pack. "Got two extra days work. No sense leaving eighty-five bucks lying on the table." The brothers take a few steps and wrap up together. "Good to see you. Been too long." The men unwind slowly, the intimacy and fondness obvious.

Heath aims a finger at the new woman in his life, sitting and watching. "Ellie McGee, meet Tick, the younger."

The woman pushes up and offers a hand, firm and callused. Two strangers, a male and a female, touch and release, friends now, accepted, no questions asked.

"Like looking in a six-foot, hundred and ninety pound, grey-eyed mirror," she says. Ellie marvels at the duplicate image.

"Twins," she decides, pointing a finger at Heath, "and you're older."

"Fourteen minutes. How'd you guess?"

She aims a smile at the question. "No guess. You told. I listened ...'Tick, the younger', you said. Makes you older. Gotta use both ears."

"Damn cold night." Tick unrolls a sleeping bag and slips inside it, scoots up and leans his shoulders against an oak trunk, bites into an apple he swiped off a tree on the way in. He tosses one to his brother. Ellie snags it in mid-air, removes a pocket knife, cuts the apple in half and shares with Heath.

Tick blows out a breath and shuts his eyes briefly, then bites into the fruit again and chews, reviewing his day, glad he'd found his brother so quickly.

The woman settles herself in close beside Heath, soaking up body heat between them. Tick reads infatuation each time Heath looks at Ellie, but reads convenience each time Ellie looks back. Protection and release, the physical needs these travelers desire, and Heath fills both requirements. A temporary companion in her mind. A pairing that suits Heath forever if he gets his way, but a partnership only for the moment in Ellie's mind. Impossible telling the future in either case.

Ellie nods her chin at Tick and says, "Odd name, Tick?" Her voice light and trim, like her body. Sensual, breathless and interesting rolled into one unkempt package. A few reddish curls hang out the front of her hood. She wears no make-up. Patches of dirt and grit hide a plain and unremarkable face until her smile lights it up. Eyes as blue as the winter sky investigate this new acquaintance, a duplicate brother. She needs a bath though, Heath too.

Heath says, "Pa named him after the highway patrol officer in his favorite television show. No one ever called him Broderick though, too many syllables for us kids just learning to talk. And Mom insisted we leave off the first part. That term 'broad' on all those mafia and crime shows didn't sit right with her so she broke off the front and just called him Rick." Heath grins. "Lucky she named me first, left Pa out of it."

Tick pokes in a sentence. "About the time we hit two or three years old, Heath kept trying Rick but it always popped out Tick due to some oddity in his speech triggers. 'Tongue training,' the doc called it, but he probably made that up just to say it, sound smart, and charge a fee. Dropped off naturally about time we turned five but the name stuck and everyone still called me Tick just to keep things simple."

Tick laughs briefly, "And me, the brat kid getting even. I kept calling him Teath." Another quiet chuckle. "Mom wouldn't have none of it though, stuck soap in my mouth every time she heard it, so I quit and rescued my taste buds."

Over near the burn barrel, a feminine titter rattles into the night once more. "Ha," Annie laughs aloud, "the brand new one-step Gator diet. Take a shower and lose ten pounds." More group laughter.

Even Gator joins in, a true realist. Then he adds, "Sure like the sound of your voice a lot better with your mouth shut, Annie." The back and forth sarcasm ignites another round of giggles.

Tick rolls his eyes left and stares between the trees. Three scraggly men and one thin as a stick, line-faced woman huddle near the fire, four derelicts sitting cross-legged on the dirt, hunched in toward the warmth.

The thin woman just lost a bet. Greta claimed she could pop the cap off a Coors bottle with her one remaining tooth. That bet won her a few beers here and there at times, but tonight that last soldier finally gave up and lies in the dirt, ignored and now worthless.

Greta takes a blood-soaked rag out of her mouth long enough to say, "Well, that damn tooth was in the way what I gotta do sometimes to git meal money anyways." Her deep south Alabama twang nearly lost now in the hollow pink smile from which her words emerge.

She tucks the rag in between her gums and suddenly groans, the shock gone, a sharp pain slipping in unannounced. "Saved a hundred bucks on a dentist though."

Her pals release a few chuckles, acknowledging the irony, but her humor fails this time. A grimace adds a twinge of discomfort to a hard life and pulls her face into an aged look she's not truly earned yet in real years.

One man reaches inside his parka and withdraws a pint, tosses it across the flames. Greta catches it one-handed, unscrews the cap, removes the rag and tips up the bottle, swishes the smooth brown liquid around a few times then swallows. Eases the pain and disinfects the bleeding gum in one slick motion. "Can't beat that sweet burn," she grunts, tips it up once more then caps it, tosses it back.

"Thanks, Alfred." Greta refolds her bandage, finds a cleaner spot, sticks it between her gums and bites down. Alfred swallows the final sip and tosses the bottle into the burn barrel. Holes punched in its bottom allow air in, ventilates the flames properly and the coals burn much hotter, reforming the glass bottles into interesting shapes and configurations.

Born with brilliant artistic vision, Greta gathers the pieces each morning after the fire cools, and makes her living decorating the deformed green, brown, and blue glass, and sells the objects at swap shops and art outlets across the nation. Aluminum cans work the same way, but the remaining small droplet-shaped metal needs a little glue, color, and creativity to make a design of any value. She fashions small silver critters dotted with colorful spirits that represent the diversity of wildlife she finds during her travels.

The moon peeks out from behind wispy cloud-cover, lights up a large metal culvert half-buried in a muddy creek bed running alongside the camp. A wooden structure spreads across its middle a few inches above the highest water-flow that tumbles through it whenever a heavy rainstorm hits.

Junkie Harrison, a long-term camp resident, scavenged a couple planks and a few branches and pine boughs months ago, laid them inside the culvert at that widest arch just above the high-water mark. Mostly it stays dry, but runoff splashes through its bottom beneath the wooden frame whenever a storm drops its load while blowing its way northeast. The make-shift bed sits high and dry. His personal waterfront estate, Junkie calls it.

Nick-named for the auto salvage yard where he once worked years ago, Junkie settles atop his clap-trap bed frame. He tosses and turns a bit, fluffs a towel under his head, getting himself comfortable for the night.

County road crosses over his culvert, and the spur line too, but the boxcars haven't moved in weeks. Junkie says he feels safer inside his curved metal house. He ignores the engine when it rumbles overhead, sporadically moving boxcars around the spurs, dropping some off, hauling some out.

'Don't hear so well anymore' he tells folks that ask.

He lies though, got superb hearing, was a sonar expert in the navy. He just trained his brain to ignore the farm trucks passing over that patched-crack blacktop and the intermittent track noise the engines broadcast over the side rails.

One time, a particularly heavy flood washed him right out, bed and all. Junkie flapped around in it for awhile, got soaking wet, and finally hauled himself up on the embankment. Lucky for him it happened during spring rains not winter or he'd probably frozen stiff. He owns no extra clothes.

Junkie wears all three sets at once, rotating one inside the other every few days, allowing the breeze to blow off that internal stink. It never works, but he rotates the clothes anyway. Something to do, keeping a schedule such as it is, in his own mind at least, counting down to nothing. He owns three t-shirts with the same message printed across the front and always readable. It announces 'God only created a few perfect heads - upon the rest he grew hair' - a proverb that fits Junkie exactly, his shiny bare scalp often covered with a knit cap in winter and a Cubs ball cap in warmer seasons.

Back in the woods and still wrapped in his bag, Tick pulls a bandana down around his ears and straightens his old Boston Patriots hat, ignoring the soft murmurs and passionate groans of a sexual union that rise above the bushes behind him. The ad hoc partnership enjoys shared warmth and the false security these brief couplings provide. Heath Simmons and Ellie McGee alone in the wilderness, enjoying a cuddle afterward.

Suddenly, the murmurs become low, angry words Tick barely makes out. "Git away from it. Leave it be or we'll come back and hurt you bad."

A few slaps disturb the peaceful harmony and then a solid thump, and another. One more thump, hard and heavy, like a bat busting a melon. Tick pushes through the brush toward his brother and Ellie. A fist arrives out of nowhere and flattens his nose, splits a lip and sits him down hard.

"Stay down there tramp, this here ain't none a yore business," a stranger snarls.

Aggressive in life and not a man that takes orders well, Tick slides sideways and kicks out. The heel of his boot connects behind the left knee and drops the stranger straight down. A loud yelp cuts into the darkness. The man swings a heavy wooden dowel wrapped in tape, catches Tick on the hip as he rises and it knocks him down a second time.

Strong and fit despite his lifestyle, Tick twists sideways, grabs a hold and wraps his arms around two thighs then works his way up. Both men wrestle for a good grip, squirming around in the pine needles and mud, too close in to punch and cause any damage.

The struggle continues for half a minute that seems like an hour until Tick incidentally traps two fingers in his mouth, bites hard and shakes his head like a bulldog on a bone-thief. Knuckles snap and crack, skin splits open and leaks blood. The stranger drops his weapon and screams. Tick pops up and kicks the man twice in the shins, once in the crotch and doubles him over.

"Yup, my business now, ain't it?" Breathing heavy, adrenalin pumping, anger pushing hard, Tick grabs the dowel and swats the stranger once and cracks the wrist on the same hand he bit and bloodied. Another swat bounces off a shoulder, and a third lands a glancing blow on his tailbone.

The stranger scuttles away beneath the brush and yells, "Let's git outta here, this guy's fuckin' crazy."

Sonar-trained ears pick up the squabble. Junkie lifts his head and watches three males dressed in black scramble through the woods and disappear, one limping and cursing, another one holding a red rag against his cheek. In the distance, an engine fires up and gravel clatters inside fender wells as a brown Ford pickup spins a horse-shoe turn and heads toward the suburbs.

Junkie rolls off his nest, climbs the embankment and watches the truck cross over his home. Brand, model, color, and year he notes automatically, all that time he worked in the Wreck-Right salvage yard built a habit. Junkie memorizes its license plate, climbs back into his house and writes the details in a notebook. Nothing dull about Junkie, despite his less than sharp appearance.

Tick wipes the blood off his face and lip, takes three steps into the woods, stops and listens. Nothing. He starts a chase then thinks better of it when the sound of that engine revs up and trails off into the distance. He spots his brother lying in the dirt.

Ellie holds his head in her lap, balls up a handkerchief and puts pressure against a deep gash on his forehead. Bright red fluid leaks around it, runs steadily down his cheek, and drips onto his shirt.

"Not as bad as it looks," she says. "Scalp cuts always bleed a lot. I'm more worried about the knot above his ear. It's swelling pretty quickly, turning dark."

Tick drops down on a knee, "Heath, open your eyes." No response, silence. "Talk to me. Come on brother, talk to me. Open your eyes."

"He's unconscious, needs a medic," Ellie says, "You too, looks like. Got blood all over your face. Go tell Annie. She burrows into the brush right behind the woodpile. Just call out her name, tell her who you are."

Tick takes two steps, turns back and kneels again, confused, looks at his hands, looks at his brother, says his name again. "Heath." A bit of fright taps into his brain, worms itself inside and scares him.

"Go on, Tick. Hurry! Tell Annie!"

He jumps up, angles past the culvert and down toward the burn barrel, trips twice in the dark, sprawling in the cold mud. He picks himself up and yells, "Annie ... Annie," and wakes everyone.

A few stick a head out, a few tunnel in deeper. All wonder what's in the works, but remain silent. No business of anyone but those directly involved. The way of camps like this, leave it alone unless it's yours. Help if it needs you, but not until asked. Private stays private.

"What? Damn it, what? Just got to sleep," a female voice groans. Annie crawls out and pops into view behind the stacked wood. "What?"

Tick explains briefly, "... some jerks beat up my brother. Heath needs a medic."

Annie stares a few seconds, "Yeah, you look just like him, 'cept for the split lip and bloody nose you got."

"Come on." Annie trots over and squeezes in next to the culvert, tells Tick, "Give Junkie a dollar."

"What? Why?"

"Just give him a dollar. He'll call the EMT's. Only cell phone here. Junkie guards it, hides it he thinks, everyone knows where though, ain't like he got a large house. It's got a little solar charger. No one touches it without asking and paying. Belongs to him. You gotta pay for the minutes."

"You use it, costs a dollar so Junkie can keep it active. Gotta call home, you put up or shut up. Just like E.T." Annie giggles, but then quickly turns serious again.

"Git on up here Junkie, emergency time. Bring the phone."

Chapter Two

Double doors marked SURGERY swing open and a dark-haired, heavy-set woman in green scrubs hurries through, looking around. Walks directly up to Tick and says, "You must be the brother? I'm Doctor Barnett, the ER surgeon. Call me Lucy."

"Yup, that's me, Tick, Heath's brother. And Ellie here, his girlfriend. How is he?"

"Still unconscious. Lots of bruising, lots of swelling. We cut in and drilled a couple small holes through the bone above his left ear and released the pressure. He was bleeding inside the skull. We drained the blood, reduced the swelling, but can't tell you when he might wake up."

Her look turns deadly serious, she touches his arm. "Or, even if he will. He's hurt pretty bad. We shot x-rays but can't tell enough from it. Looks like a fractured skull, two places and radiating out. Will do an MRI once we stabilize him a little better."

She looks away for a second. "We're all adults. To be honest, it's touch and go from here. We can only wait and see. He's on a twenty-four hour watch, and a monitor."

"Read the admit write-up. Some nasty people did this ... Sheriff catch them?"

"Not yet ... But we will." His tone implying if the cops didn't, Tick would.

Lucy hands Tick a card, her name, phone and email printed across its face. "Hard to get me, but I'll answer eventually. Just leave contact info, I'll get back to you soon as I can. We're a small ER and urgent care clinic. We stay very busy here. Get all the outlying areas, farms and ranches. Only two doctors, one surgeon, that's me, one P.A. and three nurses, but very effective and well equipped."

She cracks a smile. "We even have a veterinarian on call. We get prize animals in pretty often. Got a stall in back equipped with surgical equipment for large critters. One-stop shopping for all your bumps and bruises, pets and livestock too."

Ellie says, "Can we see him."

"Maybe in a couple hours, he's still in the O-R, then up to Intensive Care. Cafeteria's in the basement while you wait. I'm really sorry, wish I had better news."

* * *

Tick bites the end off a roast beef on sourdough. Hot mustard stings his tongue. "Whoa, that's right spicy." Ellie slides in across from Tick and nibbles at an egg salad sandwich. Steam rises above two coffee cups set between them. Pleasant cooking odors fill the room, a thing neither encounters often in the wilderness camps.

Ellie breathes it in deeply, recalling Granny McGee and her baking. Cookies and apple pie, hot rolls, the sweet, juicy flavors delightful and often just plain gooey. "Smells like Granny's kitchen out at the farm." She picks up the sandwich. "Don't taste near as good though."

"So, what's this about, Ellie? Who are these guys?"

Ellie pulls herself back into the moment. "No clue. They just showed up. Told Heath 'stay away from it', and slapped me a couple times, then used that heavy stick on him." She turns her eyes away as she speaks, as if afraid to tell it all, as if withholding a truth. "I cut one pretty deep on the cheek, and the wrist." She eases out the four-inch Buck knife, shows it, hides it away.

"We'll see a nasty scar on him if we find those guys."

Tick stares across the table. "Stay away from what? You're holding something back," he says, as if reading her mind. Ellie shakes her head, eyes turned down. "Give it up, Ellie."

Her eyes suddenly fill with tears and spill over. Ellie wipes her cheeks, "He did it for me." Tears flow freely now. "He did it for me, and now he's hurt. He was no part of it, didn't deserve this." She grabs a napkin, blows her nose and wipes her eyes.

"A free spirit, living on the road, enjoying life." A sob shakes her body, then another. "We've been traveling together a few months." More tears.

Tick says nothing. Lets Ellie work through the emotion, holding his own pain inside at the same time.

"Heath never talks much about his past," she says. "Tell me first. I need to know." She huffs in a couple deep breaths, calming herself.

Tick tells it first but knows he'll get his answers later. "Heath loves camping, the outdoors, and vagabond traveling. He quit college after a year, and spent the next year backpacking all over Europe. Came back when he ran out of money and joined the Air Force. Did some kind of investigation work, but just accounting and supplies, nothing dangerous. Not like he was a cop or a spy, nothing like that. When he got out, he spent a few years just hitching rides around the country. Ended up back home in Boston."

"Needed to refresh his bank account last year, so picked up some work with a local private security firm, evaluating records for a large national bank, not law enforcement ... 'A Temp', he called it. Haven't talked to him in awhile before today."

The emotion drains away while she listens. Ellie finds her voice again. "The bank down-sized the contract, he told me, and the company let him go. He hit the road again. We hooked up at a camp near the Finger Lakes in New York. Heading south for the winter, but he insisted we stop here, so he could 'look around' he said, for me. Been here just over two weeks. He knows Junkie and Annie from before, other trips."

"Right. Left a message with our sister, told me to meet up here, or head toward Florida if I got here too late. There's a camp north of Tampa where we met up last year. We got some harvest work in the fields, lasted a few weeks."

"He was gone a couple days, just got back a day before you showed up," Ellie says. "Knew you were coming, but not exactly when. Wouldn't let me go with him. He said he needed to sneak around, and he knew some people here. People he worked with at MacDill air base couple years ago."

"Told me to watch for you. Said you look alike, not like a mirror though." A brief grin slides across her face, then slips away as quickly as it arrived. "Let's go check on him first. Then you get my story, all of it."

Tick taps the elevator button. "You'll tell it, Ellie." An order, not a request. They ride up two floors and find the nursing station.

"He's still out, probably at least until tomorrow," the nurse says. "Doc's keeping him down, give his brain a chance to heal a little and reduce the swelling."

"Come on Ellie, we better head back and get our stuff. No telling how long it'll be safe there. Junkie probably hit us for another buck just for watching it."

"No he won't. He's a bit flakey, but a tough old watchdog. He won't let any one get away with it. Besides, it's worth a dollar keeping it safe."

Chapter Three

Next morning, the hobo camp looks the same, a few minor snow drifts in the shade, but mostly mud and brush and dry grass. Only six traveler packs remain. Most of the drifters took off for the southern states or maybe the west coast earlier in the day. Gator watches Annie strike a match and fire up newspaper and dry kindling. She builds a stick teepee above the miniature flame.

A peek into the culvert reveals no Junkie. "Rode his bike into town," Annie says, "How's Heath?"

"He's hurt bad. Won't know much more 'til tomorrow," Ellie says.

Tick raises his voice, so the few remaining can hear. "Anyone see anything last night? Know where those guys came from, or who they work for?" No response. The toothless woman and her male companion each show a negative shake of the head, and continue packing. Greta and Alfred, ready to follow the sun tomorrow or the next day.

"Ask Frankie." Annie points across the clearing.

A lean, muscular man sits in the sun and folds up a military long-coat, places it on his sleeping pad. Months of wrinkles and dirt decorate his faded green fatigues. He flips over and pushes up and down on his fingertips, his left calf crossed over his right, his left foot missing. At the pinnacle of each pushup, he exhales a near silent count. He rolls onto his back, bends his knees, and begins sit-ups. Once again the count puffs out at each lift, touching the opposite elbow to kneecap.

"Wait 'til he finishes prayin' or he won't talk," Annie says.

"That's praying?"

"Man can call it what he wants," Alfred barks, a little belligerence in his words, defending his campmate from a stranger. "His life."

Frankie unrolls his coat, pulls it on then limps along a path winding toward the trees. His right foot appears normal, encased in a scuffed military boot. Shorter than normal, his left leg swings out and lands on a cloth pad layered with several filthy gray socks.

The veteran picks a tree and locates a broken limb at eye level, imagines it a stub nose. The bark swirling around it paints an artistic face in his mind. He straightens his spine, pushes out his chest, salutes then begins. Low angry words emerge. "Ain't goin' back. Hurts. Ain't goin' back, need a foot first."

He calls it his bedtime prayer, but performs this ritual frequently, both mornings and afternoons. Roots out of his blankets once in a while at night and prays in the moonlight as if he'd forgotten it earlier. His hands and arms flap in continuous circles, like sticks on puppet string.

Frankie aims his words at the oak stub face. "Ain't goin' back. Hurts. Ain't goin' back, need a foot first." He cocks an ear, listens to the stub face. He argues with his tree, refusing its orders. "Ain't goin' back. Hurts. Ain't goin' back, need a foot first."

* * *

Frankie got blown up in Panama during an unauthorized Special Forces excursion into drug territory. Not exactly unauthorized, orders came down from somewhere, someone higher up or it'd never happen.

His six-man squad breached a drug lab. Frankie caught a cluster of nails and broken glass in his left foot when a modified mine exploded beneath him. Three men died on the spot. Captain Frank Cooper and Sergeant Jacoby Klyne executed the drug security team in an intense fire-fight, and burned the lab. Jake hid the body, no choice, and planned on sending a retrieval team in once he got back to Tango Detail.

Sergeant Klyne field-dressed the foot temporarily and carried the captain out over a shoulder. Took three and a half days. The foot got infected and, two weeks later, amputated above the ankle.

Upon his discharge, the veteran's clinic issued Frank Cooper a wooden prosthetic, an older model that supplies discomfort, redness, an occasional blister when the protective pads slip out of place. But it works, gets him around. Sometimes, he forgets the fake foot, limps around on the too short stump.

Whenever Captain Cooper passes a Veterans Hospital or an outpatient clinic, he heads on in and signs up. Gets an appointment a month or two in the future, but never returns. Too busy traveling and surviving to wait that long. Loses track of dates and time anyway. No phone and no mailbox, he receives no reminders. The constant delays make treatment difficult if not impossible for many veterans, especially homeless drifters.

* * *

He waves his arms back and forth. Balanced on his remaining foot, tilting a bit to the right side, Frankie stands at attention facing the tree. His left pant-leg hangs four inches above the dirt, empty.

"Ain't goin' back. Hurts. Ain't goin' back, need a foot first."

Frankie salutes the face, turns his back on the stub nose, limps across camp, curls into his blanket, and falls asleep immediately, his task complete.

"Ask him when he wakes up," Annie says.

Chapter Four

Ellie and Tick spend a half hour collecting their belongings, pack it neatly. Then Ellie spends another fifteen minutes searching the brush for a missing earring, one of the pair Heath gave her last night. She finally gives up, temporarily.

Ready for a quick departure, or stay over a night or a week. Depends on what the day brings, or the news about Heath. Tick carries the gear over and drops it near the fire pit. A little closer in than last night. A little safer. Ellie follows and drops her backpack beside Tick, companions in tragedy. Both rub their hands together over the small flame.

Tick says, "Okay Ellie, tell it." Annie sits in too, and Gator. Frankie rolls off his sleeping pad and sits beside his new buddy. No sign of Junkie.

Ellie tells it. "We lived right here, outside Chicago. Lost my mom in hunting camp. Dad's best friend accidentally shot her, then a month later, shot himself. Couldn't take the guilt. My dad tried at first, but couldn't handle it either, wife and best friend gone in a flash. He started drinking. Got abusive, mostly verbal. Nothing physical."

"The person that once was my father vanished into an emotional hole and never recovered. Eventually, lost his job, couldn't pay the bills. We lost our house. He just dropped me at the apple farm, drove off and never returned. No clue where he is, even if he's alive. Got a card at Christmas the first couple years, then nothing since."

"How old?" Annie asks.

"Fourteen when it happened, sixteen when he left. A rough two years."

"My grandparents took me in. After school and weekends, I helped them work a small apple orchard in the next county. We did all right, Gramps worked hard, saved a bit of money. About two hundred grand over the years, his retirement, plus he had no mortgage."

"Granny met some guy named John Reardon at Bingo, a guy preying on seniors, turns out. He invited her to his investment seminar, and sucked her into his scam. They put up fifty grand, a test, got a nice return for five months. Put up another fifty, got a nice return again. Every month just like the calendar, interest popped into the bank account. Free money.

"Eventually this Reardon guy talked them into mortgaging the farm and investing that and the remaining retirement cash. They wanted me to succeed, pay for college, make it worth all the work I did helping run the orchards."

Ellie stops speaking, chokes up. A few tears leak out.

She takes a deep breath. "I tried to talk them out of it but they did it, the whole farm and the retirement savings. Two months later, the money stopped, and we found the investment office closed, deserted."

"Local bankers Granny and Gramps knew for years tried to work with them, but no use, the title was tied up, 'a cloud on it' they said and a heavy mortgage. And the legal fees too high to fix it, and the time it takes. Eventually they lost everything." Ellie wraps her arms around herself, bows her head, her entire body shaking with emotion at the retelling, reliving her family tragedy.

"Had to drop out of college during the third year. I tried to work and help pay it, but the nut was just too big. Gramps tried too, but he was past retirement age, and worn out physically from a life working the orchard, and emotionally from all the stress. They now live on Social Security, in public senior housing. No apple blossoms in that air, just the smell of disinfectant and old clothes need washing."

No one speaks, just takes it in. Most everyone on the road carries a hard-luck story around with them, some tougher than others. And everyone on the road survives it, or not. Annie gets up and puts her arms around Ellie, pulling her in like a lost daughter. "You go after the rats that did it?"

"We never found out. We tried, cops tried at first, but the company had corporate owners, and more corporate owners, then an offshore company owned that one. We had no money for lawyers. Tried the FBI, but we had no evidence, just a misfortune for us the agent said. Thomas Hargrove, 'Don't call me Tom', he told us, 'it's Agent Hargrove or Thomas'. Kind of a frumpy jerk."

"We found the offices, a sham storefront, but mostly just one guy, Reardon, came around in person, real friendly, until he got all the money. Another guy on the phone, Mitchell, gave us instructions a few times. Then we never saw him again, phone went out of service. The fake mortgage originator filed bankruptcy, closed its doors. But the company and the names were fake, even the court papers. We got a notice in the mail, but no one ever actually filed it. Just a delaying tactic 'til they got away."

"That's it. Granny and Gramps moved into senior housing. I had no job, not one I wanted to keep anyway, working in a chain department store keeping the books. No future unless I invite the manager into my pants." She bows her head. A slight shudder runs down her body. "Fat chance." Ellie shakes off the memory.

"So I just took off, tried to make it out west, and found I enjoyed the road a bit. Partnered up with another woman for the first year or so, got some experience. And two's better than one for a lot of reasons, especially with women. Two years later, here I am. Come back here when I can, when the weather's good, visit Granny and Gramps, take up the search again."

Everyone chews on that story, taking it in, feeling it like a part of their own.

"Went to Maine to visit a college friend when she got married. Met Heath in New York on the way back. Told Heath the story. He decided he'd go investigate. He did some account security stuff for that bank in Boston. It's not the same, but he knows some people here, some Air Force buddies, and he started looking around. Maybe he got close and they didn't like it, and sent these goons to stop him."

Ellie blinks tears out of her eyes again. Another sob ripples down her body. Annie holds her tighter, letting the emotion drain away, a mother hen. Finally, Annie lets her loose and says, "Looks like Arnold's here."

A chunky, silver-haired rancher driving an old rattle-trap pickup stops directly over the culvert, engine burbling like a tweaked out hotrod.

Annie says, "Sweet sound ain't it. Like a dragster warming up on a Saturday afternoon. Junkie heads on down once or twice a month, eats a fine home-cooked meal, and tunes that old Chevy like a high-tech race machine. Fair trade."

"You two go on. Me and Frankie can ride in tomorrow, or Friday. Gator don't need it." Annie giggles, wiggles her nose at Gator, "Well, needs it but won't go."

Confused, Tick spreads his hands wide. "Go where?"

"Arnold stops every couple days when heading into town. Gives a few of us a ride over to the state park. We wash, fill water bottles. No showers though." Annie tells the story, knows the most about everyone. The state park runs a snowmobile trail and a cross-country ski track, so it's open all year. Lucky for us it heats the restrooms."

"Come on, Tick. Time for a weekly bath," Ellie says, and grabs a nylon day-pack. "Get your towel and tooth brush. I got soap and scissors, and a squirt of Colgate."

The rancher honks the horn, twice, then once, then twice, his hurry up warning.

"Only takes two or three at a time so the rangers don't complain and kick us out. He brings us back after an hour or so, after he does his business in town. Was once a traveler himself, spent summers and fall right here in this camp. Arnold gits it," Annie says. "The other option, hike across to the creek and carry everything. We hike over sometimes, or accept the ride. Creek's pretty cold nowadays, and starting to freeze up."

"Arnold found a woman owns a small horse ranch down the road a couple miles, settled in. Ain't traveled in years, but he comes down and sits with us on some warm nights. Brings a hunk a meat or a chicken, and a bottle. We down a few shots and cook up the meal, tell a buncha funny lies."

"Nice guy. Misses the road he tells us, but likes the ranch and Sue Monahan more. Even married her, or maybe she married him. Made him sign a lot of papers, releasing her property. She loves him, but knows he feels the call of the road once in a while. Sue ain't taking no chances. Smart woman."

"Arnold makes everyone ride in the back." Then Ellie and Annie laugh in tangent, both spouting the same words, a duet. "Says we all smell worse than his goats."

"He's lyin' though. Ever smelled a billy-goat? Ha, wait 'til you meet Barney."

Junkie pedals across the roadway, climbs down the bank and chains his bike to a steel hook inside the culvert. Annie heads over, chats a few minutes, and returns. Junkie follows. "Tell 'em," Annie says.

"Got the truck plate last night. Seen 'em leaving."

"Why didn't you tell me then?" Tick barks, cutting a little edge into his words.

"You wasn't in no kinda shape to listen. More important you take care of your brother. Heath comes first. Got all month to go find them assholes."

"So, who owns it?"

Junkie holds out a hand, grins. "Gimme a dollar. Had to call Wreck-Right. Jack Connors looked up the plate number. It's a rental though. Only got the rental company, can't get who rented it. Maybe later."

"Well ... we can go ask, call the cops took that report at the hospital and find out."

Frankie speaks up. "Maybe call cops, maybe not. They never do much. Hard to prove. Besides, if you ask them, you get a record of asking. You go after those bastards and hurt them then the cops will know, and come after you for it. You lose, not them."

"Okay then, how do we find out?" Ellie asks.

Frankie says, "Wait, gotta ask the Captain." He stands up, limps over to his face tree, mutters a few questions and waves his puppet hands for a full five minutes.

"Tell you tomorrow or maybe next Tuesday, or Friday." Frankie says.

Annie and Junkie look at the dirt. No one believes Frankie. He acts a little soft in the head sometimes.

"How can an oak tree talk?" Tick asks the rhetorical question, gets no answer.

Frankie frowns at the comment, then limps back to his bedroll, sits and breaks out a snack, beef jerky and crackers. He woofs it down, chugs an entire bottle of water. Glances over at Tick and Ellie and Annie. "What?" He grins. "Arguing with Captain Cooper makes Frankie hungry."

Tick takes Ellie by the arm, leads her away, out of earshot. "Well, so much for asking Frankie. Ain't the sharpest knife in the drawer, is he?"

Arnold honks again, revs the engine. Ellie says, "We better get on up there."

Chapter Five

A local newsroom fills the top two floors above a thrift store. The building stands just off the highway twenty-six miles north of the hobo camp. Sitting in a cluttered office on the third floor, Scott Monroe cleans his wire-rims, slips an end behind each ear then runs his fingers through a mop of curly blond hair.

A short, balding stump of a man with a rim of steel wool hair cut short above his ears and a sharp inquisitive mind wheels in through the extra wide door and rolls behind his desk.

"Hey Matt." Scott spins two color photographs across the desk toward the investigations editor and publisher.

Twenty-two years ago on a whim and a daydream, Matt Hoffman received a work-training grant after injuring his spinal cord playing college football. He founded an investigative news journal covering local financial issues, then expanded nationwide ten years ago, the first exclusively online money magazine. Bank Notes publishes once a month and adds occasional special editions or highlights when a big story hits. It still operates out of the same building where it was born. Every financial guru in the country subscribes. No splashy advertizing rag here, comfortable in his own niche, Matt pursues truth to its end no matter where it takes him. A good solid publisher.

Scott follows the photos with a green folder, leans his fit runner's body back in the chair. "Our guy goes by Timothy Watkins now. Not sure if he's the same crook we tracked in Milwaukee last year. Only info we have includes a description before he disappeared, no photos. Used the name Jason Mitchell then. We'd just gotten our investigation started when he split."

"What all have we got?" Hoffman asks.

"Five-foot eleven, fiftyish. Blond receding, wears it long. A little heavy, he walks every morning from what we know, but just around the block so he can tell the ladies he works out, maybe." Scott grins. "Guy likes high-end liquor and loose redheads, fast cars and fancy restaurants. Dresses stylish, tailored suits but casual, no tie, likes a hat, even during summer."

"How old is this?"

"The photos, three days."

Most of the background, twenty months or less, a little deep background two or three years. We picked this guy up again a week ago. Terri thinks he's the same guy. She's picking identical financial scam stuff off the grapevine. No real proof yet. He's careful, knows what he's doing. Nothing in his real name, which we don't know at present. All his scams run through fronts and false I.D, and he uses agents. None of his victims meet the head honcho."

"Terri got a tip, picked him up leaving a restaurant, shot these and jumped on his tail but lost him in traffic. He hot-rods a silver BMW like he's racing NASCAR."

"FBI was on him briefly a year and a half ago, Agent Thomas Hargrove. Once our aka Mitchell took off, they put this on a back-burner. Told us they'd keep it open, and are sure he'll show up again. They'll pick it up if the guy ever surfaces. We think he has, and is using the name Watkins now, and might be running local scams."

"Agent full-of-himself Hargrove won't do much for us. He's pretty lazy, not much ambition, thinks he's a hot-shot Eliot Ness though. But if we break something worth it, we might get Brenda Davis involved."

Hoffman laughs out loud, "Heard Agent Brenda made district supervisor, his supervisor. Must tweak every hair on Hargrove's head. She'll deflate his balloon in a hurry. She's a good agent and no nonsense, a real leader."

"Wouldn't mind working with her again," Scott says. "Easy on the eyes too."

"Keep it in your pants, old man, you're married now. With a toddler."

"And happy." A brief chuckle spills out.

"Okay. Stay on this for another couple weeks. Spread the word around to our other sources and agencies that we're looking again, pass a photo around.

See if we can pick up anything else, even older info might fill in some blanks."

"Right, will do." Scott picks up the photos and the file.

"At the very least, gather all we have from anywhere and create one file, cross reference under both names. If we don't get much now, we'll revisit it if we do later."

"Keep the file green for now, if we find nothing new after a month, tag it red again but don't kill it."

Chapter Six

The current three-unit office suite needs maintenance, rents cheap, and requires no long-term lease. Carlton Emory masquerades as Timothy Watkins and runs his investment scam, bilking seniors out of retirement savings and mortgages. His firm rents a new set of offices and invents new names each time a client rebels and the regulators or investigators get close.

Emory slips into his personal slot and shuts off a new black BMW 535i sedan. He steps out of the chill and into the lobby, nods at the security guard. "Harold."

"Morning, Mister Emory. All quiet today," the thin, elderly man responds. "No papers served since Monday. Two whole days. Are we moving again soon?"

Harold uses the man's real name, Emory, instead of the continuously changing names the men choose each time the scam blows its cover and moves to new offices. He can't remember well, attaching a series of new names to his old associates confuses his mind. Never a bright man even earlier in his youth, his brain's winding down now with age and alcohol. But Harold's known Carton Emory for years.

"About a month, maybe sooner." Emory continues down the corridor and enters his private office, drops his slightly overweight bulk into a fancy leather chair behind a huge custom made Rosewood desk and flips a switch, barks into the intercom. "Reardon, get in here."

Less than half a minute later, his top salesman, office manager, and partner combined pushes the door open and steps in carrying three file folders.

Emory says, "What's up with that Ingles mortgage? You fund that yet? They were hanging on that final string, so we need to cut it and deposit the money."

Reardon flips open a folder. "Meeting them Friday ... one-thirty. Should get the money then."

"That's three days. Go now, get it done. Don't give them a chance to rethink it, or ask anyone else. That sneaky son of theirs almost screwed us out of this one, got a little too nosey ... Numbers?"

Reardon runs his eyes down a page. "Gave back ten thousand five at fifteen hundred a month on the initial hundred grand. That's at eighteen percent, seven months." He flips to another page.

"They have another hundred grand cash in the bank, plus one ninety-six when they mortgage. It's already approved. So we can get another two hundred ninety-six Friday, and we'll give back another eight grand if we do the standard three months interest then kill it."

"I'll sweeten the pot with a four grand bonus if we need it to close. They'll think their account holds an even four hundred grand then. That bonus always seems to kick that last little greed button on anyone that waffles."

Emory punches the numbers into a calculator. "So, we keep roughly three hundred seventy-one and change. Not a bad take for ten months."

"Okay, do it today. And ask Rita James if she got the agreement signed on the new office suite. We need to close this one down in the next month or so and get out of town. Warming up a bit here. Damn process servers know this place now."

"Done Boss."

"Don't call me boss, sounds too mafia, like a criminal or something." Emory smiles at the comment. The image of himself as a mafia don he finds amusing and a truth, Vito Corleone or Tony Soprano in-person. Although in reality, he lacks the mobster professionalism, and remains simply a low-life but high-paid cheat.

"What about Anderson and Richards?"

Reardon opens another folder, and a third. "Anderson's only two hundred forty, and Richards about three hundred twenty. As usual, we'll get the first fifty grand from each to lock it in. We'll net about five hundred thirty-four if we run the same game as Ingles. We've got two more months on both, that'll give it nine months on each."

"Okay. See if you can move either one up. We've got two months left here, so we'll close it out from the new offices if you can't. We'll get out a month early at least. Water's getting a bit hot here and the law's nosing around. Damn subpoenas multiply like fleas on a hound. What about that tramp investigator snooping around?"

"Sent those three farm boys down a couple days ago to kick his ass, warn him off." Cliff shrugs at it, like it's handled. "Nothing to worry about. Cost three hundred bucks, cheap labor. And that tramp's never seen us face to face."

"Do everything in person on these next two. Just you John, leave Cliff out for now. He can stay on the tech stuff. We'll leave no phones or email trace once we relocate. Same as always. Tell 'em all we're remodeling next month so they don't show up here unannounced after we move out. Anyone sees this place vacant will surely get antsy about the money."

Emory pushes up out of his chair, pours a drink and shakes his head. "Fuckin' lawsuits have been hitting here two months now. Hard to hold them off, even with Martin Sloan helping. Gotta close out the accounts and ride on out of here."

He swallows the brandy and grabs his coat. "I'm heading down to EATS and get a bite and a drink."

* * *

A ten-minute drive finds a silver BMW 335i swinging into a combination bar and restaurant a few miles north of the state park and town hall. He drives the silver coupe when he's hunting, and the black sedan for business. He the parks under a neon sign that reads 'EATS 'n DRINKS' in large capital letters. Nothing fancy, but good meals and a tall pour makes the place popular with the local crowds, mostly ranchers, farmers, and working family folks.

The bartender sets a tumbler on the bar, drops a couple ice cubes, pours Dewar's over it, adds a splash, and slides it in front of the end stool. Carlton Emory sits like he owns it, and he very nearly does.

"Thanks, Gordy." The men chat a moment. Gordy moves along and fills a few orders. Emory glances around, sees a middle-aged woman with little extra weight around the middle sitting alone at a table. He waves Gordy over, signals with a finger.

"Miranda Fulton, divorced, two grown kids, and works at the Food Stop market as a cashier."

"Send her a drink." Gordy obliges, and the waitress sets a drink on the table and points to Emory. The woman smiles at him, lifts the drink in acknowledgement and takes a sip. Emory looks at Gordy, holds up his hand, five fingers extended. Gordy shakes it off. 'No bet, she's right up your alley."

Emory picks up his drink, wanders over, and speaks a few words, then joins Miranda at her table.

* * *

Two hours later at almost the exact minute Emory escorts Miranda Fulton out to his BMW for a short ride back to his rented condo, John Reardon sits on a stuffed chair across from Ida and Leon Ingles. He fabricates a comment each time the couple asks a question.

Thin, almost skeletal, a few gray strands stretch across his balding scalp. Leon Ingles rests both hands on a cane he holds upright between his knees. A light breeze might blow him out the window. His wife plops down beside him. A solid gray bun tops her head, and she spreads out on the couch like too much apple pie topped with vanilla ice cream and chocolate syrup.

Leon Ingles struggles with his voice, and finally clears his throat. "Thought you said this rate was good for the whole month?" Another hacking cough rattles his lungs.

"Well," Reardon says, "we can't control the banks. It's better for you if we get this done today. Distribution rates change this afternoon when the banks close. You'll get less per month with a rate reduction, and pay a higher mortgage."

A complete lie masquerades as truth and slides out of his mouth with no remorse. John Reardon has not an ethical or moral bone in his body. Matches Carlton Emory exactly in that respect and Cliff Porter fits the same mold. Three of a kind, perfect partners in crime, not a scruple among them.

"We can do this paperwork first, and I'll drive you to both credit unions and back. We'll collect the checks, and I'll record the mortgage after I drop you off at home."

His wide eyes and a wrinkled forehead insinuate it's too obvious to pass it up. He cracks a sly but false smile and opens his hands, palms up, as if

'Why not? It's a great deal'. He gathers the papers and quickly shuffles them into new piles.

Leon says, "Explain it once more, so Ida gets it," implying he got it. Not a chance.

"Okay. You invested fifty thousand with us, then fifty more. That gives you a hundred thousand in your investment trust. We pay eighteen percent, and if you close the mortgage on your home with us now, today, invest that two-hundred ninety-six and add it to the hundred you have with our firm, we'll back date it to the first of the month for the entire amount."

Reardon slides a fabricated appraisal and rate page across the coffee table. "Rates go down today at close of banking hours, see here," he points at a series of numbers. "So you'll drop to fifteen point nine. And, the mortgage rate goes up to seven point eight too, so your income drops about nine hundred a month and your mortgage payment goes up about one fifty. So, your total net income per month will drop. Roughly a thousand less, give or take."

Leon and Ida examine the page. The figures make no sense. Intentional. The husband and wife switch eyes back and forth between the statements and Reardon, the pause stretches into a minute, then two. Ida says, "We should call Michael."

Reardon quickly deflects the notion, "We can do one thing more. Any investment today over two hundred thousand total gets a four thousand dollar bonus directly from us, so we make our quota this month. That goes away tomorrow. Makes your investment a nice round four hundred thousand and that bonus earns interest at the same rate." He jerks the line and sets the final hook. "Back dated a month."

"All right. Let's do it today, get it over with. You'll drive us, John?"

"Yes, of course. You won't regret it." Reardon takes an arm and helps Leon stand. The scam investor hides his smile behind a serious expression, and opens the door.

Chapter Seven

Arnold rattles up and idles on the road above the culvert a moment, the small block engine rumbling out its duel exhaust like the fine-tuned machine it is. Junkie definitely earns his meals. This old Chevy needs a little body work, but its engine purrs like a well-fed kitten.

Tick and Ellie each toss in a backpack, climb into the bed and hitch a ride. Arnold swings into the state park six miles down the highway. Both hop off, salute a thank you, head in to clean up and fill water bottles.

Twenty minutes later, Tick steps outside, finds Ellie freshly washed and combing out her thick red curls. She aims a smile at him. "Feels good to be clean again."

Dressed in a dark blue tee-shirt with no sleeves she'd tucked into a pair of patched blue jeans, the tight fitting top defines her curves and proves she's a woman. Two tiny buttons poke at the fabric in the chill air, providing clear evidence she wears nothing beneath it for support. He admires her feminine qualities for a few seconds, suddenly realizing what attracted his brother to this vagabond woman. Tick's never yet seen her outside two sweatshirts and a heavy coat before this very minute.

Ellie catches his eyes tracking her moves and turns her back. She quickly adds two more layers of bulky winter clothing. Caught in the act, a little color floods into his cheeks. He turns his eyes away and busies himself dressing.

Tick recovers quickly and opens his pack, pulls an almost clean shirt out of his bundle and sniffs it. "Two days I think. This one's okay for at least one more." He pulls it over his head, then a sweatshirt and an old gray Patriots hoodie atop that.

Ellie laughs. "Yeah, got a couple here myself. We need to haul some water back and wash this stuff pretty soon, or make a laundry run into town. That little creek the camp uses all summer and fall nearly froze over last week. We'll start smelling like Gator if we don't wash this stuff ... You ready?" She gets a nod.

Each slings a pack over a shoulder. Ellie leads the way into the forest and follows a dirt walking trail. Thirty-five minutes tick off and Ellie steps out of the woods and pushes open the rear access doors at the ER clinic. Tick follows a few steps behind. Both enter the lobby and stop at a nursing station inside the main entrance.

"No change," the charge nurse says. "Lucy's in with another patient. She'll be out in a few minutes."

"She stopped the sedative yesterday. Heath should be awake now, but he stayed down. We had no reaction to stimulation, so she sedated again. She wants to keep him under, wants to be here when he wakes up the first time."

"We'll wait in the room with my brother."

Heath looks weak, pale, and lonely in the room. Pinkish splotches discolor the white gauze strips wrapped several times around his head. A double row of black stitches seals a cut above his eye and the surrounding tissue appears red and swollen.

"Looks like a mummy with a headache," Ellie says as a tear builds in her eye and runs down her cheek.

A breather tube hangs in the corner of his mouth, and an intravenous line with an injection port runs into a vein above his wrist. A plastic bag drips fluid into the clear feeder hose connected to the port. Nasty bruising runs across his right arm and shoulder, and spreads across his chest. His eyes remain shut. His body shows no movement except the breather tube puffing its continuous rhythm.

Lucy Barnett swings in through the open door. She checks his pulse, listens to his heart. "He's still down. Yesterday we tried to wake him. No luck."

Lucy lifts one eyelid then the other, shines a light into each. "Nothing," she says. She runs a wooden stick along the bottom of each foot. "No response. Didn't get one yesterday either, even after we stopped the sedation."

"What's that mean?" Ellie squeaks out the words, her emotions losing control.

"Too early to tell. He may wake up tomorrow when we try again. The MRI gave us little more detail than the x-ray in this case. Still shows radiating fractures. We can't tell what else might be damaged unless we go in. I'd rather not do that, except as a last resort. Could be tiny bone splinters or fragments embedded in his brain and blocking some nerve signals. Even MRI's don't give us everything we need."

A nurse carries in a tray, sets it beside the bed.

Lucy removes the white gauze and drops it on the tray then examines the skull behind both ears. "Still swollen and discolored. Look here."

Gently, she rolls his head a little to the left and then a little to the right, revealing patches of hair shaved away, and stitches and swelling on both sides.

Looks like he hit his head on the other side when he fell, something hard, a rock maybe. Or he got hit both sides with that club. We didn't see the left side damage until we got him on the table and shaved it. Too much hair and it sorely needed washing."

She glances up and finds Ellie and Tick staring, waiting for an answer to the question neither one asked yet. "We really don't know. Concussions are always a difficult diagnosis, and the brain sometimes acts in ways we can't predict or control."

Lucy injects two medications into the clear tube. "Sedative and antibiotics. We're giving him plenty of fluids, supplementing with glucose and amino acids, a few vitamins. That'll help keep his strength up."

"I'm off-duty in an hour. We'll keep him down again today, and see what we find tomorrow. We hope it heals, at least enough to wake up so we can get some verbal feedback, and check his mental clarity."

Back at the encampment, Tick wrings out several shirts and two pair of pants. Hangs them on a tree limb near the burn barrel alongside a neat row of socks and white boxers. At least that minimum heat keeps the clothing from freezing overnight.

Ellie takes a turn over the wash bucket and begins rinsing and wringing out her clothing. "Might smell like smoke after, but it's better than the alternative."

Tick wanders over, squats down and sits cross-legged beside Junkie. "So, what did you find? Anything more?"

'Not yet. Jack says maybe he can get the name, who rented the truck." Junkie turns his eyes toward Tick. "Not sure though, gotta call him back tomorrow." The eyes don't blink, just stare.

After a minute, Junkie removes a flask and takes long swallow, points the neck at Tick. "You need this, Ellie too."

Tick chugs a shot, hands it to Ellie. The flask makes one more round. Tick reaches into his pants and removes a five, folds it twice and tucks it into Junkie's jacket pocket. "This help with calls?"

Junkie pulls out the bill, hands it back. "Heath's a buddy, and your brother. We got enough minutes on tap for this. He's hurt." He nods his head up and down. "We'll find 'em." He tips up one last taste, and tucks the flask into his jacket.

Frankie hobbles over, squats down and rolls back onto his butt, lifts his left foot.

"Damn, that puppy's sore." He removes his fake foot and peels off several gray socks, releasing an odor everyone ignores. Normal for the life, just part of the game. Frankie rubs the stump, and spits out a laugh.

"Can feel my toes, just can't see 'em, I can even wiggle 'em. Sometimes, they itch." He rubs more vigorously, along the lower calf. "Doc says it's a phantom foot." Frankie giggles again. "Wonder if the Phantom wears a mask and plays with Batman."

Annie climbs down off the highway, heads over toward the group. "Just got my pension check today," she says, grinning. "And the party juice."

She unzips a pouch and pulls out two pints. "My turn." Another round begins kicking out the misery and stress.

"Wait 'til you hear this one. Met this really weird old guy down the liquor store, fillin' in for Hank this morning. He was wearin' a tee-shirt said 'Older than Dirt' across the front. Course, you know me, I gotta ask how old dirt is, right? Sure been around longer than you, I told him."

He tells me, 'Nope, it's a true statement. My son gimme this one. His grandma, my wife's mother not mine, insisted we name him after her favorite cartoon. Cantankerous old bat wouldn't take no for an answer. Who in their right mind would name a boy baby Dilbert? So we just skip the middle three letters and call him Dirt."

Annie starts giggling. "Didn't believe him. Thought he was makin' it up to git in my panties." She laughs aloud, that captivating feminine squeak busting out again.

"And so then this curly-haired teenager comes trottin' up with mud all over his face carrying a fishing rod and a tackle box. Big brown letters wrote across his shirt spelled out 'I'm Dirt'. Well, hard not to believe him then."

The first crazy story of the evening triggers the first group chuckle. Annie gets up and tosses a few sticks and a log into the barrel, warming up the party and drying out the clothes. Tall tales and laughter, the only two things keeping these drifters sane, and not always. That and a bottle, which Annie sends around the campfire once more.

Annie grew up right here local, but lost her firefighter husband too soon into a solid marriage. Backfire caught him in a blaze that burned a warehouse to the ground.

She raised two kids on a small firehouse pension and worked two jobs. When the kids rode off into other lives and marriage, Annie hit the road and lives off the pension. A true free spirit, she'll help anyone or everyone that helps themselves, knows a lot of local folks and survives just fine in the camps, travels often but always comes home, a base camp here, close to where she grew up.

Annie visits her kids and grandkids every couple months then returns to the drifter life. She's known Junkie since they were neighbor kids and they even dated briefly during high school. But she met the love of her life right after graduation, got married, and produced two children. She and Junkie remained friends, became even closer friends after she lost her husband. But both still embrace separate lives and the freedom a drifter lifestyle provides.

* * *

Arnold drops a single drifter wearing an oversize coat off at the state park entrance. Instead of entering the park, the vagrant crosses the highway, sidesteps the gas pumps, and pushes into the general store.

"Hey Shanty," the store owner says.

Shanty nods in return. "Hey Hank."

Shanty walks up and down the aisles, sticking various items in his pockets, cupcakes, cookies, a small flashlight, batteries, and a screwdriver. Two thin round loaves of rye bread he slides into an oversized pocket inside the coat, one on each hip. He carefully realigns each row of remaining stock after removing the item he wants. After about ten minutes, he stops at the front desk. "Just the Snickers," he says.

"A dollar eight." Shanty sets two quarters, five nickels, a dime, and twenty-three pennies on the counter.

Hank drops a receipt into the outstretched palm. "See you been diving in the city fountain again Shanty."

"Ya' caught me, Hank," he titters. "Don't tell Deputy Joe," and heads out the door, turns right towards the hobo camp, a six-mile walk. He peels back the wrapper, and bites into the Snickers. 'Need a little energy after all that work," he mutters, takes another bite.

Hank reaches into his pocket, removes a cell phone, and punches a speed dial.

* * *

Daylight dribbles away and invites dusk in for a brief visit before darkness drops its velvet shroud over the camp. A brown and white Dodge Charger eases into the gravel pull out near the culvert, parks and expels a deputy sheriff. Red and blue lights blink on a bar across the roof, and a gold SHERIFF emblem shines off its door. A large spotlight aims itself across the clearing.

Short, thick, and crafty looking, sometimes a little bit cranky but always fair, Deputy Joe believes justice equates more with circumstance than with guilt or innocence. He taps a Stetson into place above his ears, slips twice climbing down the icy gravel slope and carries himself over toward the burn barrel. A green reusable shopping bag hangs off one fist.

"Junkie, Annie," Joe says, nodding. "Come to get Shanty for stealing food and cigarettes, and some tools at the grocery store again."

"Over there, his regular hole," Junkie says.

Sheriff chats a bit, then goes over and calls into a patch of tree limbs growing over a cave-like hollow. "Shanty?" Joe shines a flashlight inside, aims it at a lump under a blanket.

"What?" A voice responds with an edge of grump in it, knowing what's coming.

Deputy Joe dog-crawls into the cave. Shanty sits up and watches the sheriff pull stolen items out from beneath a towel and an old coat. Deputy Joe drops cupcakes, cookies, two screwdrivers, pliers, a small knife, four batteries and other miscellaneous items into his green bag. Leaves rye bread and peanut butter, two bottles of cream soda.

Hank figures bread and peanut butter staples are his small way of helping without allowing Shanty to victimize him every weekend. Plays out as a bi-weekly ritual, sometimes monthly instead, like a dress rehearsal with everyone assigned a role.

Deputy Joe arrests Shanty once or twice a month for shop-lifting. Shanty goes to court the next morning, gets one overnight in jail, two meals and a shower. He's generally harmless, but an obsessive thief.

Hank learned years ago that if he tries to stop Shanty he'll pitch a fit right there in the store and upset the cash customers. His routine reeks of obsessive compulsive and anal retentive behavior. Shanty always steals the same items, as if he reads a check list in the back of his brain. Always carries everything back and hides it under his towel and coat, eats nothing but the Snickers he bought. Like a religious ritual each time it happens, Deputy Joe drives over packs up all but the rye bread, peanut butter and two sodas, and hauls Shanty in for a night.

"When you gonna learn, Shanty. You think Hank don't recognize you and what you're doing every time you go into his store. You buy one Snickers and look like a fat sausage walking out carrying all this stuff."

"Maybe I outta wear a mask. Could borrow one from Frankie's Phantom." Shanty hangs his head, grins, "You taking me in Joe so I kin git a shower and a couple meals."

A regular part-time job for Shanty, stealing from the store, getting caught and serving a day or two in the county jail. He loads the staples in an old Coleman cooler, seals the lid. "Keeps critters out," he says, pulls on his jacket, crawls outside the cave, pops up the hoodie and hides his face.

"Hold the cameras," he yells, raising his hands out in front. "Hold the cameras," like a high profile criminal case. "No photos please!" He cackles loud and long then follows Deputy Joe over to the campfire.

Tick looks at Deputy Joe and Shanty, confused.

"We all have our issues," Annie says. "Shanty keeps to himself and don't hurt no one." She shrugs, "Just the stealin', but he don't git away with it so no one cares much."

"Hank knows. And we all buy stuff from his store when we git money. Comes around, goes around. He helps us out once in a while when we're broke and Hank's known Shanty all his life, Deputy Joe has too."

"Yup. Shanty grew up here, but spends a part of each year in North Carolina too where he lived part-time with his dad after the divorce. Split custody, summer and fall here with his mom, winter and spring there with his dad."

"Winter's been pretty mild this year, so he stayed here late but will head south soon. His parents have long passed but Shanty keeps repeating the ritual, both the interstate transition and the stealing. It's like that OCD the shrinks talk about won't cut him loose. Shanty finds comfort in repeating the ritualistic behavior."

Junkie interrupts."Got any news about that assault?"

Deputy Joe says, "Nope. Nothing new. Fake ID, fake credit card. Paid cash. Phone number's a dead burner. We tracked it to a fourteen-year-old kid off a video. He told us a guy paid him ten bucks to buy four phones at Radio Shack with a buncha paid minutes."

Ellie says, "Didn't the kid wonder why the guy didn't just buy phones himself?"

"He's a kid. It's ten bucks." Deputy Joe waves it off.

Junkie grabs an arm and pulls Joe aside, huddles up. He relays what Jack Connors told him. Joe confirms the information and shrugs, says, "Probably some tramps just trying to rob Heath and we'll never get closer to finding them or solving it."

That contradiction makes the truck rental and tramp-robbing sequence irrational. Nobody rents a truck to rob a tramp. But Deputy Joe has nowhere else to go with this investigation at the moment.

Tick, Ellie, and Junkie know a little more about it, but withhold that information for the time being. They plan on sharing it once they gather a bit more intelligence.

Shanty leads Deputy Joe up the slope, a little hurry in his step. "Come on Joe, getting cold out here, and I missed lunch today. Just ate that Snickers."

* * *

Grumbles and moans greet a radiant sunrise streaking the treetops on an unusually warm morning for this time of year. The encampment rumbles to life, glad the snow flurries disappeared overnight.

Always the first to rise, Annie stirs up the coals and dumps a bundle of sticks and a log or two into the barrel, starts the percolator bubbling.

Frankie barks, "Yes sir!" salutes, flaps his arms in the puppet dance one final time, unzips his fly and drains his bladder behind the stub-face tree, aiming carefully at a bush. "Can't piss on a Captain," he mumbles. He limps back over to his sleepin pads, begins a workout, lays the left stump over his right calf and starts his fingertip pushups. A sharp 'huh' count breathes out at the peak of each rep.

Annie looks up and watches a dark gray Tacoma ease into the same spot Deputy Joe parks in each time he arrives. A gravel pullout widens the road near Junkie's culvert, convenient and enough space for a vehicle or two whenever guests arrive, or the cops. A blond-haired stranger climbs out and stretches, ambles down the slope toward the camp and offers a friendly wave as he approaches, testing his welcome.

Still in his bed, Junkie watches the stranger approach, ready to jump up if Annie needs help. Tick and Ellie sit up on their sleeping pads and study the new arrival.

The stranger walks up to Annie and asks, "You Ellie McGee?"

"Nope."

"You know her."

Annie says, "Who's asking?"

"Scott Monroe. I'm with Bank Notes, a financial magazine. He offers his card, Annie ignores it. Scott looks around, a little awkward, holding the card in mid-air.

"We're researching a story about mortgage fraud. We heard someone in her family got ripped off a couple years ago. Would like to speak with her. We think they might be working local here, and want to take them down. Make sure they don't do it again. She might know something that can help us. This company preys on seniors, mostly, steals their savings. Nasty dudes."

"How's that? You're a writer not a cop."

"We investigate financial fraud, sometimes get information the cops don't or can't get. We work with the cops too, and the feds, share resources. We're a little less restricted than they are, legally. If we get any info, they can use it to bust the crooks."

"Don't know her," Annie lies, protecting her friend until she asks Ellie personally.

The look on his face tells anyone watching he knows Annie's lying. "Okay, but if you do find her or meet her on the road please give her this card and ask her to call me. Collect if she needs it." Annie accepts the card this time, sticks it in her pocket.

"The Monahan ranch down this way?" He points southeast.

No reason to lie about this answer, it's a ranch. Not very mobile. "Yup, Sue Monahan, couple miles." Can't hide that truth, but she mentions nothing about Arnold.

Scott spins in a slow circle, glancing at each pile of rags or blankets hiding a drifter. He watches Frankie flip over and begin a sit up routine, sweat dripping off his brow even in the chill.

The investigator has no clue what Ellie looks like, or her male friend, and has no name for her companion, just heard she was traveling with a male. "Okay, thanks." He heads back up to his truck, fires it up, and continues along the highway.

Tick and Ellie approach the barrel, and Annie. Ellie asks, "What's that all about?"

Annie hands the card over. "Says he's investigating mortgage fraud. That you know someone was a victim. Your family, he told us." She points down the road. "You want to talk with him, wait on the highway. He'll be back this way in a few minutes. He drove down looking for Sue and Arnold, but they went into town today. Saw the truck pass about sunrise."

True to her prediction, after ten minutes the Tacoma appears in the distance aimed back into town. Ellie flags him down and Scott pulls over. "Ellie McGee," she says, points at Tick. "Tick Simmons. Annie said you're looking for me."

"Yes, absolutely. Thanks for stopping me." He peeks at the clipboard on the seat." Gina and Mickey your family?"

"Yes. My Granny and Gramps. What's this about investigating mortgage fraud?"

Scott turns to Tick. "Simmons? You related to the guy that got beat up a few days ago? Lucy Barnett's taking care of him at ER." He gets a nod in response.

"Can we talk? Can I buy you late breakfast, early lunch?"

"Never turn down a free meal," Ellie says. She and Tick wave at Annie then climb into the Toyota. Tick hops into shotgun and Ellie fits her shapely bottom neatly into the rear jump-seat.

* * *

Fifteen minutes later, the trio slide into a booth at Tiny's Cafe, about three miles past the state park. "So what's the story?" Tick asks, curious how Ellie relates to the investigator's work. Ellie already knows a part of it but offers nothing.

"Was the mortgage guy named Mitchell?" Scott leads into an interview.

Ellie says, "Uh uh, you first. Tell us what you know and then what you want from me ... us."

Scott shrugs. "Okay. Our staff picked up information from several sources that indicate a local mortgage company selects seniors that own a home free and clear and have retirement cash. It uses some tech method we haven't figured out yet. Then it offers a good interest plan if they invest. It pays out high interest then convinces them to mortgage the home, and invest that money too."

"At that point, it pays out the interest for a couple more months then disappears. The scam bumps up against the legal system after about a year or eighteen months and people start complaining when the payouts stop. It rolls up its rugs and moves on ... finds new victims, opens a new office under a different name. These scammers change names and locations like we change socks and underwear."

Ellie and Tick glance at one another. Ellie says, "Every three days," and both crack up. Scott looks puzzled for a few seconds. Neither one explains the joke.

Scott continues. "Everything's fake, but it takes that long to figure it out. Bank Notes, our news journal, tracked one individual with at least two names running the scam in at least two separate areas over the past three or four years. Our team watches for the scam details, and we're still trying to find him and his real name. Cops and the feds want to bust him but the complaints come in after he's already gone, or he splits right after the subpoenas hit."

A slim waitress carrying a perky smile and about thirty years experience, sets a large tray on a tripod next to the booth and delivers drinks, sandwiches, and chips. Adds a pickle to each plate. No one speaks until she leaves. Scott grins while watching Tick and Ellie speed-eat. A learned response to food on the table and slim pickings on a hobo journey. Grab it and eat it, exhibit our cultural etiquette later.

Ellie looks at Scott staring. "What?" she says then reddens slightly, recalling her long-lost table manners. The vagrant lifestyle grows quickly on its members and turns into habit with little effort.

"Nothing."

Scott continues talking between bites. "We'll get more info soon, but the name McGee popped up when we talked to Deputy Joe. He remembers seeing it in the hospital record when your brother Heath got hurt, listed Ellie McGee as his friend. Joe knows we have that last name in our records too, as past victims. It just hit him when we were talking about financial news the other day. Same last name."

"So, his name was Mitchell?" Scott asks his original question again.

No hesitation this time."Yes, but Granny never met him, just spoke with him on the phone. The other guy, John something, came around and did all the talking and signing. We never saw Mitchell."

"John Reardon." Not a question, a statement.

"Nope," Ellie says, that's not the last name. John's right though."

"If it's the same crooks, and we think it is, he's John Reardon now, and Jason Mitchell calls himself Timothy Watkins. We don't know his real name yet."

Ellie then explains all that happened to her grandparents, but adds little new information. The hit and miss scam has been hitting and missing for years, and moving, and never been caught.

Scott pays the tab, writes his personal cell number on the back of a card and hands it over.

"Let's keep in touch, and see if we can dig up anything more. Come on, I'll drive you back."

* * *

Tick and Ellie join the group and hunker down beside the burn barrel. A few show flurries accompany the departing daylight. "Getting cold," Ellie observes, wrapping up tighter.

"This keeps up I'm gonna head on down to the barn and convince Arnold he needs another tune-up. Get to sleep in a loft above the horses while I fix his tractor and ranch equipment. Usually takes about as long as it snows." Junkie chuckles at his ingenuity.

"Get any more on that rental?' Tick asks.

"Jack Connors, owner at Wreck-Right Salvage, says the rental guy won't give up the name. So, I told Deputy Joe all you told me, and to ask him unofficial like. Instead Joe bulled his way into the office, told the rental company he'd get a warrant if he needs it, and then he'd check all the records for compliance, more than once and come back again if needed." Junkie chortles, a low masculine snort like a pig enjoying a mud bed.

"The guy bent like a Chinese nail, gave up Richard Everett as the renter. Joe ran the name. Fake papers, fake everything, fake license, fake credit card, fake phone number, fake address somewhere in Idaho."

"Sounds like the Invisible Man, remember that show?" Junkie glances up at the sky, recollecting a life history, different times. He pulls himself back into the moment.

"But the rental guy told Joe he was real. Tall, thin guy with black hair. Looks Italian.' Junkie roots around in his brain a minute. "Probably mafia," he concludes.

"So," Tick says, "we're still in the same boat. No way to find these guys."

Frankie speaks up. "Captain Cooper told me okay, he'll help you find him."

Everyone ignores that offer. "What does a tree know?" Junkie adds.

Frankie looks over at his tree, squirms a little on his seat. "He knows."

Tick changes his mind, grasping at anything. "Did the tree give a name?"

"Ain't a tree. It's a captain. Army intelligence," Frankie corrects Tick. "Nope, no name. Just told me okay, and to find out for y'all. Need a phone call though. Can only get him at midnight."

Frankie stares at Tick a full minute, and finally, "Well, give Junkie a dollar so the captain can call tonight."

Tick now feels like a sitting duck on this one, too late to back out and hurt Frankie's feelings. He hands Junkie a single dollar bill. Can see it now, a tree making a phone call, poking the buttons with a sucker tip, tapping out Morse code. Tick shakes his head, the frustration evident.

* * *

A few minutes before midnight Frankie salutes the face tree. A full moon lights his way down to the culvert and he shakes Junkie awake. "Phone."

Junkie opens his eyes, points a finger at the bike seat. Frankie spots the cell, carries it outside the culvert and parks himself on a tree stump. Exactly midnight, he dials a number from memory.

It rings twice and a female voice answers, "Tango Detail. Zero, seven, one, seven, one, nine, four, four."

Frankie speaks a sequence of letters and numbers, listens for a few seconds, hangs up. Two minutes later, the phone dings once. He hits the answer button, listens again. He disconnects and dials a number, begins a conversation that lasts four or five minutes, walks back down to the culvert, and wakes Junkie again, clicks the speaker so both can follow it, and hands him the phone.

"Talk, Junkie. Everything you know about Heath and Ellie, and the rental."

"Hello, Captain Cooper," Junkie says, playing along. A male voice responds, "It's Sergeant."

"Opps, okay Sergeant, sorry." Mystified, he stares at the phone in disbelief, first that Frankie called anyone real, and surprised he hears a human voice then wonders how the captain fell backwards into a sergeant. "Go figure," he mumbles, then alternates talking and listening for a few minutes, finally hands the phone back.

Frankie says a few more words, "... my friends, Jake, they got ripped off and beat up. Ain't fair ... Okay." He disconnects, punches a series of numbers on the dial pad, then lays the phone on the bike seat. He limps back up the hill, crawls into his sleeping pads and falls asleep immediately.

At sunrise, Annie, Tick, and Ellie listen as Junkie explains the midnight phone call. "Look at this, no record of the call, it's erased. Nothing. A blank slate since you called the hospital yesterday. How'd he do that?"

"Well, Frankie's a bit weird, a few screws loose. I mean, a talking tree and all," Ellie says, as bewildered as the others.

Chapter Eight

Carlton Emory watches the movers roll the last file cabinet up the ramp and tie it off inside the box truck, then slide in the final two boxes. A few minutes later, the truck heads down the highway toward the new office complex Emory leased a week ago, another false name. He turns to his security guard and says, "That's it, Harold. Last day for this one."

"Right. Done here, Mister Emory, or is it Mister Bailey now?" Harold already knows the answer. The city fired Harold Bunny ten years ago for extorting prostitutes and low-level drug pushers on his patrol beat. He cashed in a few favors and served no jail time, paid a big fine but will never work for a public agency again.

He grew up defending himself when every kid on the block called him "Bugs" and laughed at him, offered him a carrot. Got tired of the Playboy bunny jokes too, and other noise that inconsiderate people aimed at him. Turned him into a mean, disillusioned cop who preyed on anyone he could, and abused his position in the Chicago police department until he finally got himself dismissed.

Emory offered him work immediately. A call screener that knows enough about the law to sort, forward, or divert calls as necessary, and lie when required. Harold fits in fine here.

During fifty-six years of life, Harold Bunny embraced no morals or ethics. He cares only for his paycheck and nothing about the wheeling and dealing, nor the frequent name and location changes that occur with this employer. A crooked cop works well with crooked scammers.

He lacks scruples, just like his managers, and tucks a bottle in under his desk that he sips during his work hours while he reads gun magazines. Helps pass the boring days. This company supports no walk in business, just takes the hustle directly to the residents and banks where they deposit savings. Each disposable phone call routes through the junction box mounted at his desk.

Harold answers most calls, and deflects any negative inquiry until he consults with Emory, or one of two managers. On the infrequent days when a client shows up and insists on scheduling an appointment, he mans the doors and verifies identity, makes an appointment the manager always breaks later.

The company men do business only at the residence of the victim. Any strangers show up here, he dismisses and sends away. He logs in and signs for documents and packages. A jack of all trades, as slick and devious as his bosses.

The man temporarily called John Reardon angles into his parking slot outside the office building. Emory greets Reardon as he enters and hands his partner two large envelopes.

"New ID, John. Cliff too."

Both men enter the offices the company will abandon today, a month early on the lease. Process servers know this address and show up too often, bothering Harold with legal trivia, subpoenas and such. Court orders to supply documents and other financial evidence, which Emory ignores.

Cliff Porter finishes shredding a set of documents, drops the ribbons into a small metal container and lights a match, watches it burn down, then carries it all into the restroom and flushes the ashes.

Emory says, "Did you guys both dump the old ID's?"

"Yeah," Cliff says. "Just finished. Shredded, burned, and flushed same as always."

Cliff sits and clicks open a desktop. "Fished up three more names for you John."

"What kind of numbers?"

"One fifty cash, mortgage about two hundred. Second one about the same, little more cash. Don't have the nuts for the third one, but will get it later today."

"John's got the new ID package. Cliff Patterson and John Randle, same first names as usual. Call me Rich Bailey, for now at least." All three crooks emit a chuckle.

Changing names almost as often as they change shirts, it makes sense to keep the same first names so no one accidently forgets when interviewing a victim together. Emory never meets a client face to face personally, only on the phone, so his new name only matters when he shows it for a lease or hook up utilities, or other temporary legal or business needs.

Emory says, "Looks like this first one is ready today, right Cliff?"

"Set it up at four today, but we can change it 'til tomorrow if you want, John."

Reardon says, "Nope, I'll go. No sense leaving our money in her bank any longer than necessary." Another devious snicker makes the rounds. The men pick up the last two laptops and the shredder, grab a few remaining files, and lock up this office for the final time. Emory tosses the keys into a drop box outside the entrance.

*

"Missus Alexandria?" The newly named and just as devious John Randle asks when an elderly and fragile woman wearing a dark blue sweater over a granny dress answers his knock. A light lavender scent floats out the door.

"Mister Randle, I presume. Please call me Virginia." She giggles, a feminine tinkle reflecting her tiny stature and sense of humor. "Alexandria comma Virginia looks like the name of a town where politicians reside whenever I write it out on those name backward papers that keep coming in the mail." She giggles again.

"John, please," he says, and steps indoors off the porch and accepts a chair.

He displays a stack of documents Cliff fabricated this morning, duplicating the same stack he's often presented over the years. But for a name and address change and the amounts solicited for investment, the scam package remains identical to every set of documents he's offered since partnering with Clayton Emory several years ago.

Virginia says, "Every time I look at this, it seems too good to be true, and my husband, rest his soul, said if it seems too good to be true, it probably isn't real."

The fraudster shows her the fake account security notice, the federal bond guarantee, the written promissory note, and other false documents created to pacify a homeowner. Gold seals, official stamps embossed into the paper add an authentic look.

"Wilbur made all the financial decisions for us," she continues, "and now that I'm alone, it falls to me." She glances up a moment, in quiet memory of her late husband.

John runs through each document as if it really means something. "This one guarantees the federal government repays you the investment, including interest, if our company fails to perform. The promissory note provides the interest rate, and this portion," he points to a clause, "indicates the amount in this account is federally insured, so it can't default."

Mister John 'Many Last Names' plays this game so often he can recite it in his sleep. No hard sell, no pressure, he allows the mark to make the decision and believe it. Both John and Cliff run the soft push every time, and it frequently works. No one likes aggressive tactics scratching at a savings account. That kind of emotion pushes a client away, and makes it likely he or she will call a friend or professional for advice.

The threat to consult an advisor or attorney always kills the deal immediately, shuts down the sales hustle, and triggers a call the next day that aborts the qualifications of that client. 'We're sorry, but you don't qualify,' they always say. Emory takes no chances that a potential victim might alert the authorities.

Side-tracking that consult or family possibility often leads to the final offer wherein a signing bonus one day that expires the next often pads the presentation enough to seal it.

The team loses a client more often than it wins, but each winner brings in several hundred thousand dollars, after expenses and payouts that set the hook. Just a few wins and the team collects big money. Successful closings run three or four a year, and the scam itself runs eight to ten months in one location, sometimes longer, up to a year or more when everything falls right and the authorities remain in the dark. It's tough work, scamming seniors, and each fraudster invests long hours in every deal.

When payouts cease and the lawsuits begin, the company packs up and moves on, inventing new names and replacing the burner cell phones each time. Compared to most financial frauds and scams it amounts to small potatoes, but devastates seniors with finite private retirement funds.

John says, "Take some time, look all this over. Check our website. You can see we've been in business for over twenty-five years." The old website, another false ploy Cliff built with careful planning and trick technology contains a set of false reviews dating back years. He builds a new website illustrating a long history each time the group moves.

Chapter Nine

Senator Miller Winston, a staunch advocate of democratic systems and values, and a proponent of circumstantial justice. A foreign ambassador several years ago, his life once sat in default as a prisoner of the drug producing factions in Panama. After an amazing operation run through a Special Forces detail that Captain Frank Cooper commanded, and Jacoby Klyne implemented, a successful rescue. Winston no longer believes that fundamental morality exists in the human species. He experienced a prime example of that lack of morality while a prisoner for more than a month.

Winston, the youngest senator ever in the long and storied political history of Massachusetts spends more time researching and writing bills that address issues in his state than he does consuming luxury lunches or afternoons on the golf course. He arrives on time for dinner with his family as often as he can instead of attending gala events and glad-handing other politicians while they point shiny white teeth at a camera lens and extend greedy fingers toward the rectangular green paper that pads the PAC animal tummies.

Elected by the people, not the political machine, his constituents love his ideals and philosophy. 'He'll be around awhile', his supporters say, 'definitely presidential material'. Instead of spending his election funds on campaigning, he banked that money, printed one pamphlet listing his accomplishments in local politics and as an ambassador to Colombia and Panama, and mailed one to every residence in the state.

He took the balance of his election funding, salted it heavily with his own capital, claimed he was building political support in order to sidestep the campaign spending laws in a positive way, and founded a series of non-profit health care clinics for the homeless and disadvantaged, particularly veterans. The newspapers ran wild with it for days and weeks, and then updated his health care progress monthly.

No need for campaigning after that story hit the streets, and Winston won with a landslide margin wider than any state or federal election in Massachusetts history.

The senator quick-steps around his desk and wraps his visitor in a bear-hug. "Good to see you, Sergeant. Been a long time."

"Yes it has, sir, two years, and it's just Jake now. Took a discharge right after that drug camp assignment in Panama when Coop lost his foot, then got caught up in my own mess in California and Colombia." Jake Klyne drops into a seat. "Hear you swept the floor in that last election, Senator."

Winton laughs. "Swept the election, not the floor."

"Yes, we did, and it's still Miller, Jake. I just do the things I believe in first, things that need doing, so to speak. Makes no sense to blow hot air into a promise that you'll do it after an election just to win votes, and then spend a season or two looking for excuses why you can't follow through on your word." The senator flops back into his chair. "You willing to tell me about Colombia now?"

"That's why I came in-person. Want to tell you thanks again for getting me out that time. I've only been back in the states ten months, and just left D.C. this morning."

Jake begins a long and convoluted story about his false imprisonment in California orchestrated through a federal intelligence agency and its director. And a larger story when his interactions with a cocaine smuggling organization based in Colombia nearly got him executed.

A record of that odd and treacherous journey sits in a top-secret file tagged 'Operation Crossbow' at an intelligence agency in Washington, D.C. No one can get at it without the president and at least one Supreme Court justice signing off.

"So, when I got stuck with no way back into the states, another ex-pat agent hooked me up with that satellite phone. You brought me home."

"Quite a tale, Jake. You brought me home once, I brought you home once. But you're not here just to thank me again."

"No, not exactly. Remember Captain Frank Cooper?"

"Of course, he commanded the rescue squad. Got us out of that drug camp in Panama ... How is he?"

"Not well, lost a foot during a drug operation we busted up right after your extraction. My last assignment with Coop, just before my discharge. Well, his too, DOD discharged him into the VA system."

"Yes, I read a security report about that incident. Thought he received a medical discharge and treatment at a veteran's clinic in Tennessee."

"Didn't stick with it for some reason. He's been bouncing around the country ever since, homeless and mostly broke. Friend of his in a homeless camp says Coop's following orders from an oak tree. His brain got a bit fried after he lost his foot, and nearly lost his life. The oak tree told him to call me to help his friends and he did, two nights ago. Used the old Tango number, and apparently, it still works."

"Yes, I keep it operational and maintain contact with the ex-ops guys when we can, we try. Some pretty special soldiers in those units. Some lose their way."

"Yeah, well, Coop's one of them. Heard nothing from him in over a year until the other night. Call came through Tango Detail asking for me. Got back to him, he needs help finding a crook that burned his friend, assaulted him, and put him in the hospital. A real estate investment scam of some sort. Not sure if it's for real or his tree talking."

"I'm on my way back to California, but will stop in Chicago and meet up with Coop, see if I can get a straight story. Maybe help him with the VA clinic stuff. Get medical help for his foot, maybe some psyche help too. I'm flying out this evening."

"If we can assist, let me know, and tell Coop hello when you see him." Winston pushes up out of his seat. "Come on, I'll buy you lunch before you head out."

Chapter Ten

A car door slams shut up on the highway but a dreary morning and dense fog protects the vehicle and its occupant from view. The few camp residents that remain turn eyes toward the road. Footsteps crunch in the gravel, then crackle across dead grass, leaves, and sticks. A dark form emerges slowly out of the mist, and reveals an athletic male dressed in military fatigue pants, black boots, a dark blue UCLA sweatshirt, and an old Los Angeles Rams knit cap. A month old beard covers his cheeks and chin, neatly trimmed. Jacoby Klyne lifts his nose, tests the scent of fresh-brewed coffee and wood smoke.

Excited, Frankie jumps up and hobbles over, his fake foot dragging a bit, and holds out a hand, the men fist pump then chest bump. Frankie says, "You came, Jake, you came! I was worried you'd not make it." Both men touch foreheads and hug in that brothers-in-arms greeting soldiers practice world-wide.

"Told you I would. Been a long time Coop, good to see you."

"Lots of people tell me stuff. I believe it when it happens."

"Miller Winston sends his regards."

"The ambassador?"

"A United States Senator now."

"Senator, hot damn, a senator," Frankie flaps his arms, yells at his oak tree. "You hear that, Captain, a senator."

"Yeah, he is, sitting right up there in the catbird seat, one of the few that does it right. Works for the people not the political agenda."

"Good thing we carried him out then." Frankie sits, introduces his friend and military buddy. "He'll help you Tick."

Tick shakes his hand, Ellie smiles and nods. Junkie waves from his culvert.

Shanty spent the night with Deputy Joe, collecting his monthly shower and hot breakfast. Most other drifters already headed south or west. Annie nods, cooking up a new pot of coffee.

As a rule, most transients accept a friend of a friend as one of their own until he proves different. But the drifters administer a group watch any time a new arrival appears. It's the way of vagabonds, and personal survival. Jake can earn full trust eventually, like anyone else, but for now he's part of this group and Frankie carries that responsibility.

Annie offers coffee, "Black, all we got," she says. "One pancake left, it's yours."

"Thanks. Only way to drink it," Jake says. He rolls up the pancake and it disappears in three bites

"So tell me, Coop, what's the problem?"

"Get over here, Junkie, you know the most," Annie hollers.

Junkie crawls off his bunk and shuffles over, pulls a log up and plops down by the burn barrel. Brings a metal cup, pours himself a brew.

"Right, well we don't know much, but a license plate, a fake name, and three bullies that beat up Tick's brother. He's in the clinic with a busted head, still asleep after more than a week."

For the next hour, bits and pieces and guesses fill Jake in, each drifter telling a part, and interrupting, clarifying, and speculating. Filtering through all the chatter, Jake creates an incomplete but fairly accurate picture of the assault, the rental, the history of Ellie's family and the financial ruin, and a story the news investigator told.

"No magic answer," Jake says. "Not sure I can help, I don't know any of these guys or how to find then any better than the local deputy."

Annie slips a hand into her jacket, brings out a pint bottle. "This goes right nice with black coffee, and might help lubricate a few ideas, get 'em rolling around inside our brains." That comment elicits a group laugh, high fives, and complete agreement.

Only one additional but interesting piece of information pops out across the fire after three or four runs through the assault and one more bottle. Each drifter gives a personal take, including embellishment wherever possible. Ellie tells she cut the guy on his left cheek. "A pretty deep gash, slashed his left wrist too," she says.

"Shoulda told us that before," Annie says.

"Why? It's not important," Tick says, thinks about it. "Should've cut his throat."

"Tried and missed. Scratched him pretty good though," Ellie adds, looking at her fingernails.

Tick says, "I think I tore a couple knuckles open and maybe broke the wrist too, on that other guy, the short one."

Jake raises his eyebrows at hearing those new revelations, but says nothing. Just takes it all in and evaluates it as best he can.

After the night of story-telling, a bucket of hobo stew, and sharing another bottle he bought at the general store, Jake crawls into back seat of a Buick he rented. He wakes Frankie early, herds him into the Encore, fires it up and heads north toward a veteran's clinic located in the next county.

Frankie signs in for the eighth time in two years. Jake leaves him for a moment, and steps outside. He punches a code number into his cell, listens, hangs up, dials again, listens then explains. "Need a list of any knife wounds treated in any ER or Urgent Care facility within fifty miles. Also, damaged or broken knuckles or a wrist." He gives GPS data, the date, and disconnects.

After a three-hour wait to see a counselor, a half-hour search of the records, and a few phone calls, the veteran's service officer reveals the truth. "Captain

Cooper signed up for health care seven times over the past two years, made an appointment to see a doctor each time, but never showed up. He filed a disability claim once, in Tennessee right after his discharge but he never checked back in at the Tennessee clinic. We eventually logged his claim inactive."

As is often the case with no way to contact a homeless veteran, the financial office just holds it, waiting for more information on the claim. Veterans Administration could not find Frankie, nor did it look. A passive environment exists in all veteran's offices because it cannot search for everyone or even anyone. It simply waits for the claims, evaluates each one, and processes a claim when it arrives, sometimes timely, sometimes not.

Jake leaves Frankie filling out forms again in a different office at the same clinic. He files for a claims review, identity confirmation, and a new identification card. Jake promises to retrieve Frankie later, and heads out to introduce himself to Deputy Joe and Scott Monroe.

Combining the best possible coincidence with a piece of pure luck, Jake finds Scott at the sheriff's office chatting with Deputy Joe, accumulating information for his ongoing investigations including the Heath assault and the McGee financial fraud case.

Deputy Joe says, "We followed up on the tag, Jack Connors at Wreck-Right told us Dave's Rentals refused to identify the renter. We badged and barked and threatened a little extra cooperation out of Dave and he eventually came up with a name. Richard Everett. No local record."

Deputy Joe shakes his head, his irritation on display, "No license, invalid credit card, disposable cell number, and a closed post office box in Ketchum, Idaho. No forward on it, blank on all DMV data bases and our state crime base as well."

"Checking the store video downtown on State Street, we caught up with a kid some guy paid to buy four phones. Dead end there. Phone company records we got with a subpoena show a few calls logged to businesses but most in and out calls go between the burner phones," Scott adds, "and no information on that name anywhere in our files either."

* * *

Rolling south along the blacktop toward the hobo camp, Jake when his cell dings lowers the volume on Jonny Lang singing *Wander This World*. "Klyne," he says, and recites a series of letters and numbers. He listens a minute and signs off, shuts the phone.

Frankie drums his fingers to the beat and stares out the window, ignoring the call briefly, then asks, "Get anything?"

"It'll come."

Jake and Frankie drop down into the encampment and explain that Frankie spent all day at the clinic. Frankie heads over, flaps around, updates his tree then rolls into his bedding, falls asleep.

Late in the evening Jake engages in an interesting and detailed discussion with the camp residents. He learns about the grandparents, how depression set in, how much they were damaged by the financial fraud that ruined their future, the best description of the attackers, and of the man Ellie met during the fraud process when her family funds got scammed.

"John something," was all she could remember, "it's been almost three years, and that Mitchell guy only talked on the phone, never came in person."

"Deputy Joe tries," Annie says, "But he's only one person, and a night duty cop rotates from one to another station if the jail has any overnight guests." Annie aims a grin at Shanty. "One assistant helps in that small satellite office. Can't do a lot, and he has very little of that fancy new technology."

"Johnny Connors comes when Joe needs him. Stayed last night, we play checkers sometimes," Shanty spits out a giggle. "I usually beat him."

Back from his monthly visit with the sheriff, Shanty grins at Annie, listens breifly, then quotes a statement he once heard and thinks sounds cool. He finally gets to use it. "Me and Deputy Joe been friends since we was kids, and Johnny's his nephew. A good guy and a pretty straight up cop. Born right here, but ain't the sharpest knife in a drawer." Shanty cackles loudly at his own wit.

"Ha. One dull knife describing another dull knife belongs in a comedy routine," Junkie says, popping that regular group chuckle open again, even Shanty joins in.

Humor and sarcasm binds the minds of travelers, otherwise, they might all go crazy. Each one embraces laughter as often as possible, despite hard times, cold weather and half-empty bellies.

At three-thirty in the morning in the back seat of his rented SUV, a single ding breaks the silence and wakes Klyne. He listens for less than thirty seconds, hangs up, and settles back under the blanket.

* * *

Fourteen hours later, as the evening sun drops behind the treetops, Special Forces Ranger Jacoby Klyne parks his rental at the curb, slips around back, checks the alley and locates a rear entrance, then circles around front and enters a country bar called the Longhorn Tavern. He studies the room a moment. The full bar and most tables contain rural cowboys, draft beers, and a few women. Peanut shells litter the floor and a juke box blares 'Walk the Line'. The odor of working men and stale beer hovers in the room.

His eyes settle on his target. He approaches three thug-looking guys wearing dirty jeans, cowboy boots and flannel shirts. The thug triplets lean against the bar, sharing a near empty pitcher.

Jake picks out the heaviest. Flab mostly, but some muscle hides under that plaid lumberjack shirt. He notes a fresh scar and stitches running across the guy's left cheek and nearly healed scratch marks on his throat, another stitched cut on his left wrist. Jake recalls a fact, Ellie told him she cut a cheek on the one that slapped her, and scratched him, cut his arm. A second thug sports a stretch bandage wrapped around his wrist and two splinted fingers.

That's how he found the name, checking local clinic records for a cut and stitched cheek, broken knuckles or a wrist, then asking around a few places. Got the location of this hang-out, the fourth try.

Simple task, but not for everyone. Need to know what you're doing, and have a few connections you can trust.

"Your name Tank?"

"Yup. Who's asking?"

"Me." Jake waves a hand at the bartender. "Bring my friends another pitcher." Jake pulls out a roll of bills, allows the thug triplets to eyeball it, and peels one off.

"Bennie tells me you might be interested in some side work. Couple guys I know need a little convincing," Jake says.

An overworked but attractive brunette blows a lock of hair out of her eyes, carries a full pitcher of beer over, and sets it down, adds one more glass. Jake slides a ten across the bar, holds his palm up in a keep the change signal. She shakes her head, holds up the ten. "Eleven fifty." Jake shrugs, adds a five. She smiles her thanks and fills four glasses.

"Who's Bennie?" Tank asks.

"Does it matter?" All three thugs empty half a glass in one long swallow, copycat partners. Bully brains forget the initial question, and accept the free beer.

"You want the job or not?"

"Maybe." Tank looks at his buddies.

"Do we git travel pay?" The middle guy with the wrist-wrap and a finger splint adds a smirk.

Jake mentally labels this one Smart-mouth. "Nope, just a free ride to the clinic." No one figures it out. The men look at one another, offer a collective 'why not' shrug.

"Let's take this outside and talk. Too many long ears in here." Three men drain three glasses, leave the pitcher, a pack of smokes, and keys on the bar, saving the spot. The thugs strut across the room and follow Jake out the rear door into the alley.

"Okay, listen up," Jake says. "I lied. There is no job. But before y'all go turn yourselves in tomorrow and tell the sheriff you beat up my friends at the hobo camp, you need to tell me who hired you first."

Puzzled disbelief crosses his face as Smart-mouth looks at Jake then laughs. "We ain't goin' nowhere you little shrimp. Not 'til after we toss your ass into that dumpster over there anyways."

Unafraid of a challenge, a common occurrence in this arena, the thugs separate and spread into a stance filled with intent. Each mimics the others, rubbing their palms together and then along their jeans as if anticipating a little fun. Five hands curl into fists. Smart-mouth eases the splinted knuckles slightly behind his hip.

"Then we're goin' back inside and polish off that pitcher you bought. Might even buy a couple more with the roll in your pocket." Smart-mouth makes his first mistake. He turns his eyes toward the dumpster for a second or two, fantasizing, then brings his eyes back around front again, his concentration lost briefly.

Jake says, "You might ask Deputy Joe if his nurse can take a look at that broken nose you got."

"Ain't got no broke nose," Smart-mouth says. His second mistake. About the time he finishes that sentence, he grunts and his rear end hits the dirt. Blood dribbles off his chin and onto his shirtfront. Without realizing he'd already been hit twice, very hard, Smart-mouth grabs his nose and slowly topples sideways.

Balanced on the balls of his feet, Jake faces Tank and notes the scars again. "Better stop in the ER clinic tonight and tell Doctor Barnett you have torn ligaments and two fractures in your right elbow, and a dislocated shoulder."

"Whu-u-ut?" Tank says, puzzled, a little beer slur in the word. A fan belt squeals when the heat pump kicks on. Building noise and highway traffic cover the sound of two loud cracks and a horrific scream that erupts in the alley. No one else hears it.

The third and youngest punk holds his palms out in a typical surrender posture and backs up a bit, bumps his butt against the block wall.

Jake growls his next words. "You pick. Which bone should I break?"

The question spins in his brain a minute then he holds out his left hand. "Just the pinkie ... if that's all right."

"Take a deep breath," Jake advises, and gets a soft frightened 'okay' and a sharp inhale in return. Jake can't help himself and laughs out loud, ignoring the finger.

"Pay attention, all three of you. Go down to the town offices across from the state park tomorrow. Ask for Deputy Joe. Tell him you assaulted our friends at the hobo camp last week."

Ignoring the continuous moan from both thugs lying on the ground, Jake lunges forward one step, and fakes a strike. The youngest punk jerks his head back and it thumps the concrete block behind him. A urine stain spreads across his pants. The punk rubs his head, examines his fingers.

"First, tell me who hired you," Jake says once more. "I'm not asking again!" The punk pulls a card out of his pocket, hands it over. Jake reads it. "Cliff Porter."

"You all go down and tell Deputy Joe you beat up our friends at the hobo camp. If you don't show up by noon, I'll be back, and you'll never see me coming and next time, you'll recognize this night was only a teaser."

"You understand these instructions?" He gets three nods, they believe him. "Don't tell anyone we met, ever, not even the sheriff or you all end up in body bags."

Jake jogs around front and slips into his SUV. The tires slip briefly in the sand as he spins away from the curb and heads south into traffic.

* * *

Deputy Joe glances up, watches Tank and his two buddies enter his office and raise five hands in surrender. The sixth hand protrudes out the end of a full-length plaster cast hanging in a sling off Tank's left shoulder. The thug with two black eyes a nose splint and a bandaged hand says, "We did it. We beat up the hobo guy."

Without missing a beat, Deputy Joe says, "Okay, gimme your names, again." He knows these local punks. All three have been in an out of his jail on a few occasions, minor assaults, drunk and disorderly.

An hour later, each prisoner lies back in a separate cell while Joe writes up assault charges and a three single page confessions. "Go figure." He smiles and shakes his head in disbelief.

Chapter Eleven

Jake kicks off his blanket, pushes the rear door open and slides out onto the gravel patch beside the highway. He pulls on a hat and a jacket, stretches out a few kinks and a slight cramp in his calf after sleeping in the back seat. The smell of fresh coffee percolates into the dawn.

First one up as usual, Annie bustles around the burn barrel, tests the taste of her first pot today and smiles at her top-notch kitchen skills. She sets out a small wooden box. Each clan member drops in some loose change every few days, and Annie buys fresh batteries for the grinder and beans whenever she hits the general store. She grinds it fresh before dawn every morning and the residents all share it. The aroma of freshly perked coffee provides a perfect wake-up call.

"Mornin'," Annie fills a cup for Jake and one for Frankie.

Jake carries both cups, sets down on a stump and watches Frankie finish his morning chat with the tree. "Ain't goin' back. Hurts. Ain't goin' back, need a foot first."

He salutes, steps behind the tree, empties his bladder then hobbles over and joins Jake, plops down on a fat log. "Ahhhhh, Annie's coffee. Nothing tastes better in these woods on a cold morning."

"So, what's going on, Coop?"

"Nothing, Captain says I gotta go back to the VA today." Frankie rubs his head, cups his ears, and then wraps his arms around his body and squeezes, rocks back and forth for a few minutes. "They don't help much. Just talk a minute, listen to my heart, send me to see someone else a month later." He picks up his fake foot, rolls it around in his hands, examines it closely and lays it back down by his bedroll.

"I know. I'm driving you this morning, again. More paperwork."

"Okay." Frankie turns toward Jake, his eyes wide open, agitated, his eyeballs flicking back and forth between Jake and the face tree, as if choosing one or the other. "Captain said I should go with you, Jake."

"Come on, Coop, it's a tree. Trees don't talk. We gotta get you fixed up. This ain't like you."

Frankie rubs his stump. A rank odor rises off two gray socks and the pad beneath it. The outer sock needs a needle and thread. He sticks a finger in a hole, glances at Jake, grins. "Hole." Glances at the tree again, back at Jake.

"Just like Panama that one time, hole in my sock. Remember it? When we burned that pot field, and got caught in the storm getting away. Sat in a cave until the rain quit." Frankie spits out two crisp bites of laughter. "All those bats flew out above our heads. Scared the hell out of us." He looks at his tree once more, as if asking permission to remember.

"It's a tree Coop, an oak tree, it's not real. It can't talk."

Frankie stares at his friend, Jake stares back.

"It's not you, not Captain Cooper. You just imagine it."

Random thoughts tumble around in his brain. Frankie wanders through his mind, pauses for what seems eternity but the clock ticks off a mere fifteen seconds. A tear rolls down his cheek.

"I know Jake, I know. But that tree helps me think things through, helps me cope with the rest of it. Talk it out. Lets me discuss life with my real self, the self I lost. My foot, the political efforts, the drug war, the tragedy of it, the violence, the waste. Trees bring me comfort. Trees don't judge us, Jake, or judge what we sometimes did to keep this county free and safe." Another tear hits his shirt.

"Those folks judging what we do, what comes of it? Let 'em walk a mile on my stump. See what they all say then." Frankie takes out a soiled handkerchief, wipes his eyes. "Don't let 'em take my tree, Jake. It's the only thing keeps me sane."

Jake wraps his arms around his friend, a combat buddy that stood back to back with him and other Special Forces soldiers during some of the most dangerous military operations in the world. Jake holds on tight. "We'll fix it Coop, we'll fix it together."

"Ain't goin' back. Hurts. Ain't goin' back, need a foot first."

"Nobody's making you go back, Coop. No one, I promise ... Come on, strap your foot on, and we'll go. I'll buy you breakfast."

Frankie glances down at his filthy coat and pants, runs his fingers through his scraggly beard and hair. "Won't let us in. Won't let me in, you can." He chuckles briefly then a frown stretches itself across his face.

"It's okay, Coop. I'll go in and get the food. We can eat it outside on the curb."

Chapter Twelve

A Toyota Forerunner pulls into the parking lot at an old office building ninety miles and two counties away from the last one. Newly minted salesmen Cliff Patterson and John Randle climb out. The black BMW follows them in, parks next to an Acura.

"Right on time," Emory says. All three enter the new offices, and Emory greets the old standby security cop. "Hello, Harold. Like your new kiosk?"

"Great, Mister Emory. Nice new seat, very comfortable." Harold Bunny tilts back in his chair. "Phones work now, too." He points at a relay system that intercepts all calls before routing out to the appropriate partner. "Office stuff was delivered yesterday. Two new computers and a printer came for Cliff this morning."

A minute later, Emory tosses a folder on the desk inside his office. "Well, John, where are we with Alexandria?"

"She gave up the first fifty grand finally, but seems a bit hesitant with the rest, and the mortgage. Will take some convincing. Probably help if she gets a couple interest payments on this initial investment. That usually does the trick. Folks see that income, get greedy."

"What about you, Cliff?"

"Got two more names. Already printed the package. Both out of town at the moment. Visiting kids, one in Texas, one in Oregon. Thought it might be good idea to wait, so they don't talk about it with family. I'll hook John up when they get back next week. Looks like a Monday, and a Thursday."

Randle opens his briefcase, removes a promissory note he signed with Virginia Alexandria, and a certified bank check for fifty thousand dollars. He pushes the documents across the desk. "Here, smile at that one Cal. Sucked that old bat right in."

"Okay, we'll put her on hold for two months, check with her then. Maybe take her out for lunch a couple times, John. Don't try to sell her then, just friendly talk. Might take three or four interest checks to convince her we're legit," Emory says and laughs, pulls a grin out of each cohort.

A phone dings, Cliff Patterson looks at his screen. "Another subpoena filed today. Same process server trying to call in, find out where we moved. They're coming a bit faster now with all this automated banking. Investors won't listen to our excuses for mail delay and bank signature holds, and all that now. They get pretty antsy soon as we skip two or maybe three payments."

Emory says, "No problem. Court servers can't find us here. The old phones have been dead-ended for a couple weeks, and the relays will disconnect tomorrow."

Patterson slides his chair over to his desk, pops open his laptop, brings up the internet and a new search program he wrote. The search begins correlating seniors, social security recipients, large cash deposits that individuals paid income taxes on last year, and homes that have no mortgage filed with the county. "I'll run this here today, and get those new desktops up and running tomorrow. And the printer. We need to make more copies of the paperwork for these new clients, change the names around."

A digital robot burrows into secure financial programs, extracts the data and logs information that meets all three criteria then logs out and erases itself.

He hooks up a small printer while the robot roots out a minimum home value with no mortgage, at least one owner over sixty, and bank interest accumulation above a certain amount which indicates large amount of cash on deposit. A combination of values less than a specific number figures into the parameters. Less educated and less sophisticated seniors know less about investment, and are easier to convince the fraudulent investment is sound. The hourglass spins and counts faster than the eye can follow.

"Always wonder why you never took these tech skills to the financial markets and picked up a legitimate job, Cliff," Randle says.

"Got a minor record I can't shake off the wires. Believe me, I tried. Cooked the books on a real estate development a few years ago. The state regulators busted the builder, and forced me to testify or go up on state and federal charges. I gave 'em what they needed and walked away with ninety days in county jail, one year probation, and a record I can't expunge. Didn't give a shit about the builder, he was a crook anyway."

All three men laugh at that last comment.

"Besides, who wants to kiss management ass for seventy grand a year when we can make half that a month each right here."

"Learned a long time ago, this is a whole lot more fun. Getting inside these systems all these banks and records offices think are safe. One reason we don't get caught, we don't take money, just the information that identifies our new clients. Ain't the same as stealing money people will notice, we just take names and no one cares. Like candy from a baby."

John nods his head, "Yeah, well you're right about that, the pay and the fun."

The lack of character exhibits itself in everything these three men do in life, a melding of completely devious personalities. No ethics, no morals, no sympathy, no remorse, and selfish to an extreme. A perfect fit, fraudsters to the core.

The laptop pings, and the printer spits out a short list. Emory looks it over. "Fifty-eight," he says. "That means five or six possibilities, and maybe one or two of those will bite." He divides the stack in half, hands one pile to each man. "Okay, run our usual analysis, and pick which ones we go after."

* * *

Jake and Frankie swing into the clinic parking lot. Frankie climbs out and limps toward the entry doors. He cradles his foot instead of wearing it. Jake points at it and Frankie says, "Pretty sore this morning, the cold and all, rubs it raw." Both men enter the clinic.

After a two hour wait, a locked door opens and nurse wearing green scrubs and a name tag that reads 'Nancy Browne RN' steps out. "Frank Cooper," she calls. Frankie raises his hand. "Come with me." Jake looks at his watch, back at Browne.

"I know it's late. Too many patients, not enough staff." She shrugs it off. "Sorry."

Jake says, "Just curious. How do you get over an hour late when you open at eight, and fall three patients behind by nine, and it's now ten-thirty?"

She shrugs again, "Sorry, the doctor arrived late today."

"All of them?"

Frankie looks around, hoping for a tree to ask permission. No luck. Grabs an arm, "Ain't going without Jake coming too. Ain't going in that office without my friend."

Gently, Jake pulls his arm away. "Go on Coop, I'll be right here." Gives Frankie a nudge. Frankie steps a little closer. "Promise Coop, I won't go anywhere."

Nancy wrinkles her nose."What? ... You live in a barn, Mister Cooper?"

"Nope, live in the shade of an old oak tree." Frankie grins. "Don't have a shower."

"Give me that coat." She grabs the coat, hangs it in the custodial closet and leads Frankie into the staff washroom. "Off with the shirt and the pants."

Frankie looks at her, rotates his eyes around in the room. No privacy.

"Mister Cooper, I was a military nurse more than twenty years and in a combat deployment three times, and now a VA nurse for eighteen months. Believe me, I've seen more than you can imagine, and more than you can show me today. Get the clothes off ... Please." She includes a smile this time, turns her back.

She pulls a set of blue scrubs off a shelf. "Wash there, in the deep sink," she points, "and put these on. Can't do much about that hair," she says. "The doctor wants to examine you, not pass out. Come back and see me after the exam, and I'll find some soap and shampoo you can take with you. On the house," she adds a grin.

Frankie says, "Cool. On the house, like a bar?"

"No, not exactly," she says. She heads back into the waiting room, offers her hand, "Nancy Browne. You two been friends long?"

"Jake Klyne. Yeah, long time. We served together."

"Help your friend, Mister Klyne. Keep him coming back. We can help him too."

Jake reads her face, believes she means it. Nurse Browne leads Frankie into the medical office, complete with his relatively clean body and new scrubs. Just before she clears the door, she grins. "And buy him some new clothes."

* * *

Back at the ER clinic down the highway from the state park and the hobo camp, Lucy Barnett pushes the door open and enters, always in constant but controlled and efficient motion. Ellie and Tick follow her in.

Heath appears pale and unhealthy despite around-the-clock care. Stitches stand out black against an angry red scar on a near colorless forehead. His eyes remain shut and he's never regained consciousness over the past ten days. Lucy checks the vitals, peels open an eyelid, peeks in, opens the other eye, flashes a pen light into both. "Well, at least his eyes aren't fixed. His pupils dilate with the light, but a bit slower than I like to see. They've been slow since admission though so no negative change at least."

"We've stopped the sedation and tried three times to wake him with stimulants," she says. "No luck. We're thinking we should transfer him to a better equipped brain trauma center. We're state of the art here for emergency care, but very understaffed for this kind of prolonged treatment, and we have no neurologist on staff either, just a consulting team from UCMC in Chicago when we need it."

Ellie takes up his hand, rubs it gently, leans in and hugs Heath. "We're right here for you, Heath. We'll be here no matter what."

Tick takes the other hand, and wraps an arm around Ellie as well. Ellie turns to him, glances up into his eyes. Tick reads a signal, a slight flush rises in his cheeks. He removes his arm, but continues holding his brother's hand. "Hang in there bro'. We're moving you to a better place."

* * *

A Bank Note company car stops at the ER clinic entrance. Scott buzzes down his window, waves a greeting. Tick and Ellie climb in the back seat. The green Blazer heads down the highway toward the town offices. Tick and Ellie follow Scott inside for a meeting with Deputy Joe. After reviewing everything they know, Ellie says, "Well, we have a name at least. Jake gave Frankie that card, don't know how he got it and he won't say."

"We don't really care how he got it, or where. It's a start, and we've got the assault guys but they know nothing, or won't say if they do," Tick adds.

"Cliff Porter. The same name comes up a few times in several mortgage fraud investigations," Scott says. "No address or employer or phone we can find. And the office where we found Watkins and shot the photos, it's empty now, deserted."

"Right, no address, no identification in any records we can access either," Deputy Joe says. "And, nothing but this phone number, and three contact numbers lead to dead burner lines, no forwarding numbers, same as the post office box in Idaho. Called Hargrove at the FBI office. He pulled his head out of his ass long enough to admit he has nothing we don't have already."

"He asked about the broken elbow and smashed nose. The guys told us the pickup hit a tree. But we have no record of an accident, and no damaged truck. And, they arrived in a lifted farm truck registered to Tank's mom. She came and got it."

"Maggie begged me to let her visit her son a minute then slapped him silly until I grabbed her hands and pulled her away. Angry as a hornet, screaming he had no business sitting in jail freeloading when he had chores to do at the farm."

"The whole situation seems a bit strange, but all three punks tell the same story. Like a recording. They don't know who hired them, just called the number on the card. Cliff Porter gave a time and they only met twice, both times at the Longhorn. Once to get the job, once to get paid. In cash, three hundred bucks."

Deputy Joe enjoys a brief chuckle. "Hargrove threatened to pin the 'beating a civilian' on us, here at the station. What an asshole." He waves a hand at the accusation.

"Told him to bring a warrant and whatever evidence he'd manufactured. He changed the subject. Feds got no jurisdiction here anyway, even if we did it. Which, if I had my way, we probably would've. These three been troublemakers around here damn near since they first popped out of their mothers."

"Makes me wonder about Frankie's friend," Tick says."Seems pretty fit, and he served in the military with Frankie. He got that card somehow, day before these guys showed up here. I'd sure not tangle with either one, even with that missing foot. You ever watch his workout? He calls it praying, I'd call it muscle."

"Well, the military adopted a new policy, so we'll just apply it here. Don't ask, don't tell." Deputy Joe echoes his chuckle again. "So, we won't ask Jake, we'll just use what he gave us."

Chapter Thirteen

"Sit up here, Mister Cooper. Take off those socks and drop them in here." Nurse Nancy Browne holds out a plastic trash bag. "I might be a nurse, but I'm not touching those socks. Lucky you don't have fleas. Dump the pads in too."

Frankie removes both gray socks and the cloth pads. Browne examines the stump. "You don't take very good care of this, do you? It's red, bruised, and rubbed raw in places, and the pad slips around. Pads should fit tight and tie in at the top."

Frankie pulls his stump away. Tries to look at the end, but it won't bend up that way. He rubs it, and grunts at the soreness.

"What happened to the tie straps at the calf?"

"Don't remember. Must've fell off.'

"Rotted off more likely," Browne says. "We'll fix you up with some new pads today. This foot doesn't fit properly. The stump has unstable support at the attachment end. Either you broke it, or it was an incorrect fitting in the first place."

"Always been like this," Frankie says. "Since Tennessee." Under his breath, he adds, "Hurts. Ain't going back. Need a foot first."

"Going back where?" She gets no answer. "We'll take care of the foot though."

The door swings open. A tall, thin man wearing black rim glasses and a white lab coat enters. "Doctor Tuttle," he announces. He sticks stethoscope buds in his ears and pushes a stainless steel disk against Frankie's chest, listens and moves it a couple times. "Take a deep breath."

Frankie grabs the disk, speaks directly into it. "That's my heart doc. We came in here for my foot." Frankie points at his left foot. "Foots down there. Well, it ain't down there, that's the problem."

Doctor quickly pops the ear buds out and rubs his ears, looks at Frankie like he's nuts. Browne taps the doctor on the arm, points at the x-rays clipped on a light-box.

"Okay. What've we got?" He checks the prosthetic foot and the x-rays, examines a few skin abrasions closely.

"Older style prosthetic. Incorrect fit, painful and uncomfortable. A lot of raw skin and several callus patches," the nurse says. "Probably a wrong cup size and fitting the first time, too large for his calf, so the stump moves inside. Looks like this one was built for an amputation higher up. We only have partial patient records at this time."

Tuttle lifts the leg, peers at the stump, rubs it and twists it, squeezes it in a few places. Frankie pulls it away and grunts. "Damn it. It's sore doc, that's why I'm here. Quit poking it."

"Good surgeon, solid stump, no problems there. Needs a new style prosthetic. Let's get him into fitting and measure it out." He looks at Frankie again. "Takes about two months." Then looks at Browne. "Make an appointment then."

"We have two model seven-seventeen's in the medical supply room, one exactly the right size. I just checked."

"Those are state-of-the-art new. Test model for local patients only so we can monitor. Just order one, a standard seven-oh-nine. He can wait."

Frankie spits out a few words, a little annoyance showing. "What, this ain't one. I'm walking around with no foot and you're telling me some other veteran *might* come in here with a brand new cut off foot bleeding out, so you keep one on tap just in case."

"That's not what I meant. We keep these new test models in the reserves, in case we lose our supplier, and we want someone local so we can monitor it. Make an appointment in two weeks for a fitting then a second one in two months when we get it delivered." He turns abruptly and hurries out, the door swings shut behind him.

"Sorry," Browne says. "That's not how we generally handle this. But he's new, and we have a heavy turnover of doctors here. Hard to keep the good ones. Takes awhile to break them in, too, when we do get one." She shrugs her annoyance right along with Frankie. "Serving our veterans is nothing like a private practice." She spends a few minutes washing, applying ointment.

"You just told him everything. Why it's sore, what to do, what I need. Even told him you have one." Frankie cuts a little edge in his voice. "What do we need him for?"

Browne grins but ignores the question. "Here, take this tube, rub the cream in when it gets sore."

"It's always sore."

She opens a drawer, hands him an additional tube. She slips on a new pad, shows him how to fit it and tie it over his calf, hands Frankie two extra pads. "Take these with you. And wash the socks and pads out once in a while. Every day is best."

"Can't every day," Frankie admits. He hobbles out into the lobby, finds Jake, explains the visit, and the results. Tells him what the doctor said, what the nurse said.

"Don't seem right to me, two more months," Jake says. Frankie agrees. "You should've done this a long time ago."

"I know. But the captain never told me, Jake. Besides, it's getting too cold here. Will be heading south soon and miss it anyway. Two months."

"You've got to stop that, Coop. Talking to trees won't help this, and missing appointments won't help it either. Let's go see what we can do. Come on." Jake heads off to the administration offices, Frankie stumping along on an old combat boot and a new white pad, carrying his fake foot, the package of ointments, and his new supplies.

"We don't have all his paperwork. He tells us he's been in numerous clinics one time, but it takes more than that to treat and heal a patient," the clerk says.

"So, what about this treatment, this foot, a two week wait just to fit and order it," Jake says. "And, what about psyche?"

"We only do verifications here. You need to go upstairs to psyche for an appointment. And I know for sure psyche is about six or seven weeks out, or longer."

"Come on, Coop. Let's go out in the lobby, you can flip out, jump up and down, kick some chairs, roll around on the floor holding your head. That'll get you in today."

"Okay." Frankie cackles loudly and draws a curious stare from two nurse trainees walking down the corridor. "Sounds like fun, better than a freezing campsite." He limps back toward the lobby, still wearing the scrubs, and carrying his foot and gear.

Jake grabs his arm, "Just kidding Coop, come on. Let's go find the psyche ward."

Frankie tracks down Nurse Browne first, and gets his coat. "Can't leave without my coat," he insists. "Too cold, and it's the only one I got. Mine since the Army."

Nurse Browne slips some extra soap and shampoo inside the pockets, hands Frankie a plastic bag tied tight at the top. "Here, socks and underwear, your shirt and pants. Needs a washing machine, or a trash bin."

At the psyche specialty clinic upstairs, a clerk tells Frankie, "We still need paperwork for this treatment and the claim. Need medical records from Tennessee and treatment discharge papers. We have no records for you, it's your first time with us."

The claim documents sat for months in various VA offices, none coordinating with the others, and with no action because Frankie traveled around and never came back to the same clinic once he left Tennessee, his home state. He never sent all the paperwork he needs to enroll to one place, so each clinic just waited, expecting Frankie would send a complete set.

Jake and Frankie walk a verbal complaint up the chain of command but have no luck. The director that can make a decision like this one is off on a 'training session' in Hawaii for two weeks. "No one else can do it," the assistant says.

"Of course. If the director got hit by a car and was out six months, would nothing continue to happen then, too? What if he dies, will nothing ever happen here again?"

Jake curls his lips at the incompetent organizational policy that allows any veteran to sit in pain and untreated while one top dog takes a vacation. "No one is that important." Jake steps outside the office, opens his phone and hits a speed-dial button.

A tinny sounding voice crackles over the speaker. "Be quick, Jake. Got a meeting in two minutes."

"I'll need more than two minutes. It's about Coop and the VA. When can I call you back? ... Okay, nine tonight." He shuts the phone, retrieves Frankie.

"How about a motel room and a shower tonight instead of the camp?"

"No thanks," Frankie says. "Gotta go back and tell the captain what happened."

"Gotta stop that, Coop. It's a tree."

Tossing words at a losing battle for the moment, Jake watches Frankie hang his head, put a frown in place. "I know, Jake. I know."

"All right, Coop. Looks like a pretty good snowstorm coming in. We should get you a new tarp, at least. The one you have is torn. Maybe replace it with a small tent?"

Frankie perks up. "Yeah, but maybe a snow flap instead of mosquito netting like those ones we had in Panama. Half the time, those little buggers slipped in anyway."

Both agree it's a good idea. Jake wheels into Hank's place, the local market that sells a little bit of everything, a true general store. He and Frankie pick out a one-man tent, stakes, and a new sleeping pad. Jake adds a few groceries and also buys himself a sleeping bag, puts everything on a black credit card with silver letters and a bald eagle embossed on one corner.

"That single blanket in the back seat ain't gonna cut it tonight," Jake says, observing the nasty looking weather heading this way.

A light dusting of snowflakes blows across the highway, and dark cloud-cover in the distance predicts a heavy storm tonight. The Buick rolls south toward the nearly empty encampment.

Upon arrival, Frankie sets up his new canvas shelter, pulls a grin across his face and aims it toward his tree. "What's do you think, Captain? Damn sight better than waking up with a beard full of ice. Should've bought this earlier, instead of the tarp."

Frankie arranges his face and glares at the oak tree. "Why didn't you think of this? Should've told me earlier," Frankie grumbles. A naked oak branch wiggles in the breeze but offers no excuse.

Annie climbs down off the planks where Junkie lives, and greets Jake and Frankie. "Junkie lets me sleep out of the weather in his bunk when he's down at the barn for a few days tuning Arnold's truck. Was just cleaning up a little before that blizzard hits tonight."

She trades a few chores for a protected spot inside the culvert and atop those planks, while Junkie finagles a meal and a night in the horse barn in exchange for a tractor tune-up. When truly brutal cold come in, Annie and Junkie both stay in the barn, and do a few chores for Arnold and Sue, eat a few meals. And, Annie helps Sue with canning, gets a ration of the produce for herself too. The arrangement works for everyone and has been going on for years. Both Annie and Junkie are locals, born and raised close by and neighbors as children, but each a victim of a few bad breaks at the wrong time in life. Neighbors are neighbors though, especially in rural areas. So that bond lasts a lifetime.

"Long as I give his bed a good cleaning and spread some new branches around. Fair exchange and it don't take long. Sure beats that little dent in the bushes I crawl into on most nights," she admits.

Annie and Junkie share his bed together once in a while as well, when the need for physical release pops open. Neither Junkie nor Annie wants a full-time partner, but a long-time drifter relationship over the years allows that enjoyment without the usual stress that often comes with it. Good old 'friends with benefits' concept works well between Junkie and Annie, no commitment beyond the physical satisfaction and true friendship.

Jake watches Tick and Ellie pull old pine needles, dry leaves, and twigs out of the bushy interwoven cavern Shanty abandoned yesterday. Ellie says, "Shanty helped a guy move some furniture, made enough money to get back to North Carolina. Arnold gave Shanty a ride to the state park. Got all cleaned up and bought a new shirt and pants for the hitch-hike south he makes this time every year. He'll be gone the winter, comes back here every year in late spring or early summer."

Tick and Ellie gather pine needles, brush and leaves, and create a new floor beneath the canopy. They lay out pads and a sleeping bag for each, and place the clothing packs in under the natural overlay supplemented with sticks, branches, and a few canvas patches Shanty accumulated over the years.

Chapter Fourteen

Annie, Tick, Ellie, Frankie, and Jake hunker down close in to the burn barrel. Frankie stokes up the fire, kicking up as much heat as it can as the snowfall increases. Tick takes the first slug then passes around a bottle he bought down at Hank's earlier.

"Figured we'd need a little warming up with the storm coming in tonight," he says. The group reviews its failure to gather any new info. The hands on his watch tick up to a nine and a twelve. Jake shakes the snow off his shoulders and hikes up to his Buick, climbs inside hits the speed dial.

The senator answers on the first ring. "Winston here, what's up with Coop?"

"He's having a bit of trouble getting medical care." Jake explains the problem, the misfit foot, the delays in paperwork, and various clinics he tried to enroll in and failed.

"His own fault," Jake admits. "He tried several but no one at the VA ever coordinates, and he's a little dizzy in his organization skills at the moment. We know the kind of operations he led, and what that does to a brain. He's in and out of a stable mind pretty often, sometimes focused, sometimes disconnected. Keeps asking an oak tree for advice, which gets him nothing. I want to help him, Miller. He's my friend, and he earned it."

Winston says, "Yeah, me too. Been there myself, in a way. And you mentioned Coop earlier, so I had some time this afternoon. Called our district VA director in Tennessee. He sent a currier over and printed a copy of the discharge and admission records, and treatment schedule. Sent it overnight to a clinic near you, and where I know the director. It's not all there, but enough info to get him enrolled and treated."

"Vickie's tracking his trail after discharge. He's been all over, a day or two at a time, months in between, no returns. A real mess. That clinic where you took him today is not the best choice. The director's ready to retire, but looks like he's under investigation. Abusing his vacation time among other things, lack of leadership."

Vickie's an excellent assistant by the way, and pushed our authority and ordered each clinic Coop visited to collect all records and forward everything to the clinic in Chrystal Hill overnight too. Three of her and I'd get everything done we should get done and could dismiss six of my staff."

Winston laughs briefly. "Chrystal Hill's a good clinic, only been open six months or so. The medical director's an old college buddy."

"It's a half a day drive from where you are now. Take Coop up there tomorrow or the next day. They'll be expecting him. Ask for Doctor Samuel Beans, he knows you're coming. He's a good friend, a combat field surgeon early in his career, and a now great psychiatrist. He'll fix him up with the right treatment."

"What about a new foot?" Jake explains the new test foot Tuttle refused to release. "He wants to keep it in stock for a local case."

"Refused huh? We'll make the call. Tuttle will be disappointed when he arrives tomorrow and finds his favorite prosthetic foot on its way to Chrystal Hill. Might have to wait a day or so, but we'll make it happen. Take that one off your plate, Jake. Can't believe Coop's been walking around on a mistake for twenty-eight months."

"Thanks, Senator. We owe you."

"Nah, you don't. We all owe Coop and you. That'll never change. Keep me in the loop. And by the way, VA approved a claim for back disability pay for the foot."

"Almost seventeen thousand sitting in his disabled vet service account waiting for an address to send it. He filed the day he discharged. Got his approval after a few months but never picked it up nor gave an address or a bank account. Hope that makes up some for his ankle pain. He'll get a check every month now if he gets an address or better yet, an account for electronic deposit. Make that happen, Jake."

"Thanks, Senator. Will do." Jake fishes a note out of his pocket. "One more thing. Got a dead burner phone and a name, Cliff Porter. Can you do anything with it? We need to find a guy." Jake reads the number.

"Give me a few days."

Exactly as Jake ends the call, a set of headlights pulls off the highway directly behind his Buick. Red and blue blinkers light up. Jake holds up his hands and shades his eyes, climbs out. Deputy Joe Eagleton emerges out of the darkness.

"Got some bad news. Tick lost his brother this evening, couple hours ago. He never woke up. Lucy Barnett called me, asked me to drive out. She has no contact number for Tick."

"That's tough news, Joe. Tick's sitting down by the barrel with Ellie and Annie." Both men slip and slide down the slope, slick and slowly filling over with snow. The bulk of the storm hovers in the distance, but it will come in strong before morning.

Joe breaks the news, waits patiently for the emotion to rise and fall. He's no stranger to bearing bad tidings. Tears of sorrow come instantly to Tick and Ellie. Annie turns and trudges away through the snow, wraps her arms around herself, engulfed in her own personal regrets for the loss of a friend, and for no good reason.

"Was wondering when we'd know for sure," Tick says. "Lucy decided it was too dangerous to move him, and told us a couple days ago he might never wake up. The pain of waiting's almost as sad as finally knowing it's over."

Tick and Ellie wrap one another into a hug, begin grieving as one. Tick hides his pain within a stoic resolve, but the sobs wrack Ellie as she imagines herself responsible. Heath stepped into her problems and brought injury to himself, made the ultimate sacrifice. The intensity of her guilt burns her soul to its core.

"I can drive you in now, before the storm closes the road," Deputy Joe offers. "Or come get you in the morning after it clears. Make arrangements. Your choice, Tick."

"Let's go now," Tick says. He turns his head away as his eyes finally spill over uncontrollably, and his shoulders shake. "Gotta call our sister, too." His voice finally cracks and exhibits the sadness and loss he feels.

Jake kicks through four inches of old snow, squats down and pulls back the tent flap, tells Frankie the news about Heath. He explains the conversations he had with Senator Winston.

Frankie says. "Never easy, losing a brother so young. How's Tick taking it?"

"Too soon to know. He went to make arrangements. Joe's driving him, and Ellie."

Tick says, "Our sister will want services in Boston. The family has a lot of friends there, and a few cousins. I'll make the call, and take care of that today."

Frankie and Jake make plans to drive over when the storm breaks, check into the Chrystal Hill clinic, and get the treatment started.

* * *

Deputy Joe makes a special return trip to the jail after dropping Tick and Ellie off at the ER clinic. His nightstick rattles on the bars and wakes up his prisoners. "Guess what dudes? Your assault charges just turned into a murder beef. No bail. And we already got your confessions. You guys are damn lucky the governor abolished the death penalty in this state a couple years ago. Now it's life without parole."

Tank wraps his arms around his head, rocks back and forth. "What the Fuck! Mom's gonna kick my ass! I got chores."

"State might just save Maggie the trouble and kick it for her, Tank. Murder for hire now. That won't sit too well with our district attorney. You three assholes are dead meat. Believe it!"

Chapter Fifteen

In his new offices sixty miles away and across the Cook County line from Deputy Joe and the thug triplets, Carlton Emory tosses a folder on his desk. "We got a problem. Alexandria wants her money back. She says she signed the papers too quick. Didn't ask her daughter," Emory says. "A damn attorney in San Francisco. How'd we miss that on family background?"

Randle flips through a few pages. "Shows the daughter deceased. Wish it were true. Maybe we can run out to San Francisco and toss her off the Golden Gate." He laughs about it but wouldn't put it past this group to authorize a hit.

"An attorney's the last thing we need in this mix. Somehow we missed it, fished up an inaccurate record. She lives under a different name. She's married now so her new name just never got into any systems we can access or monitor." Randle drops the file on the desk and rubs his neck. "Looks like the marriage date and the deceased date are identical. Another government paper mill fuck-up."

"I took her call day before yesterday," Randle says, "Alexandria said the daughter told her to get the money back or she'll file a complaint, and a lawsuit."

"Get out there tomorrow, Cliff. If she thinks John cheated her, she won't even open the door for him," Emory predicts. "Tell her it takes a week at least to get her funds released. She'll probably buy it. Don't let her call her daughter if you can help it."

He walks in circles, thinking it through. "Tell her we fired John today and will refund her money. See if you can gain us enough time to get out of here, and lease some office space outside this county before she files a complaint and the regulators find us. A week will do it. See if you can stretch it out for two."

"John, you go out and find a kid somewhere, buy us burner phones again. Can't take any chances if an attorney climbs up our backs." Randle heads for the door.

"Damn it," Emory barks. "We just got here too. Might have to shut down for awhile. Give Singleton a call. See what else she's got available for short-term rental, month to month, no lease, no credit check, at least two offices, and a secure entry where we can stick Harold and his phone system."

* * *

Standing beside a filing bin in the county offices, Scott Monroe snatches a document out of the basket and pumps a fist into the air. Pure grunt work. A very solid and thorough investigative journalist, Scott believes grunt work gets the job done. Check files and data and official sources over and over, boring, tedious, and time consuming. But when it pays off, the reward makes it worth the time and effort. Scott discovers the complaint Virginia Alexandria filed against John Reardon one day after it records at the business license office, pays the clerk three dollars for a copy.

He dials Virginia Alexandria, explains Bank Notes magazine and his job as investigator, and makes a time to meet later in the day. Scott pumps his fist again as he exits the town hall. "Yes!" Scott hops and skips his way over toward his Blazer, climbs in and heads south toward the hobo encampment seeking Tick and Ellie. It never crosses his mind to speak with law enforcement first. Deputy Joe remains outside this loop, at least for now.

* * *

Early the next morning, Virginia Alexandria sits at her kitchen table speaking into her phone. "The finance rep's coming today. Says he'll give the money back if I want it. Says he'll explain all the options."

The cell speaker squeaks out a sharp retort. "No! Don't agree with anything he says. No options, Mom. None! We examined all the copies you sent, and investigated the charter. It's fake, it's a complete illegal rip off. I'm preparing legal documents to file with the

Federal District Court tomorrow. Wish you'd have asked me first."

"You were in France. I didn't want to bother you and Curt on vacation. And that's what the magazine guy said too, yesterday. He advised me to keep the meeting with the rep, and see what they say. I'll record it if I can figure out this fancy new phone contraption you sent me."

"What happened to a simple phone that you just dial and connect to another person and just talk? This one damn near cooks dinner and washes the dishes after." She eyeballs the flat blue screen on her birthday gift but can't figure out or use half these new-fangled applications yet, and probably never will.

"Don't tell this rep anything, Mom! Nothing about the reporter, our investigation of his company, the feds! Nothing, you hear me?"

"Yes, I hear you. Please lower your voice or I won't even need this phone. I'll just walk outside and listen."

"Get your money back if they offer it. And file a complaint just like I told you, even if they refund the money." A knock at the door interrupts.

"I filed it already, two days ago. He's here, Kim. I'll call back if it disconnects." She sets the phone on the coffee table. The green dot remains lit. The screen turns dark after a few seconds.

She opens the door and finds Cliff standing on her porch. "Oh. Where's John?" She takes no notice of the slight dip in his jacket pocket where a thirty-two caliber pistol weighs it down.

Cliff offers his false business card. "Cliff Patterson. The company dismissed John this morning. He treated our clients a little differently than we like. May I come in?"

She examines the card, steps aside, and both find seats in the living room.

"John pushes clients a little too quickly. Didn't give you enough time to think this through. That's not how we do business," he lies. "We want to make it right, make it comfortable and safe for our investors."

Virginia Alexandria says nothing, waits for more, skips the coffee and rolls she normally offers her guests.

"We feel bad about the way John took advantage. So, if you still want in, we're here to make that happen. If not, you can sign a release and we'll have your funds returned within a week. It takes that long to clear and process."

"Cleared in twenty-four hours when you took my check." She stares straight into his eyes, a little grit in her voice. A no nonsense woman when a situation requires it.

"True, but that's different. That's a deposit from a cash account, not a withdrawal from an investment banking instrument. It takes time. Federal regulations." More lies.

Alexandria keeps her anger in check, plays it out. She's already filed a complaint. "Well then, how much time?"

"Generally a week, but I can try to speed that up for you."

"Okay, tell you what, Mister Patterson. I'll give the week for returning my funds and look the prospectus over again, in more detail. If it still looks good, I'll continue with the balance and the mortgage. But your good faith gives my original money back first." She can lie with the best of these crooks, even though she has no prior experience, and no plans to review the prospectus again. She's out, period.

"We got a call at the office. John said you plan on filing a complaint against him?"

"Not yet. We'll see what happens this week." Another creative fib. She forces her lips to stretch over her teeth, but it's not a true smile, more like a silent snarl. "And, if we don't see our refund, then I will file that complaint."

"Excellent. Will call you before the weekend, or Monday latest." Cliff stands and departs the home as fast as he can.

"Did you hear all that? I just set the phone down, didn't turn it off."

"Yes, we did, Mom. Heard it and recorded it."

"Well he was so anxious to get out of here he didn't even have me sign that release he said he needs before he can refund the money. For sure, it's a fake. I'm going down and talk to the District Attorney tomorrow, and file a criminal complaint as well at the civil complaint that's already filed."

Cliff jumps into a gray Acura and heads back to share the good news with his partners. He got the week. Patterson has no clue a green Blazer trailing behind him means anything. Jake and Scott turn and face one another, and grin.

"Gottcha," Scott says, and pumps a fist. The Blazer tracks the man who was Porter and now Patterson up onto the highway and back toward his offices. The crook never looks back. The Acura just cruises along, dragging that dark green tail behind it.

* * *

Frankie sits on a log outside his tent and whittles on a one-inch thick oak stub he'd broken off his tree, carves out eyes and a mouth around a protruding knot nose, holds it up in front of his face. "Man, sure is a handsome devil, ain't it? Needs a little hair though."

He watches Jake exit his Encore and drop down the gravel slope, slipping a time or two like everyone else.

"Okay, Captain, you're safe here. Just ride in this jacket with me and Jake to the clinic, stay out of sight. Don't you say anything, I'll do the talking." He wraps a red handkerchief protectively around the stub and places it in his pocket.

Jake and Frankie climb the slope, hop into the silver SUV and head north on the highway, then east for several hours. Jake pulls into the local branch of a national bank, and Frankie opens up an account that accepts electronic deposits. He'll receive just over five hundred dollars a month for his wartime injuries. He convinces Jake to become a co-signer on it, just in case. "What if I'm in the hospital? Can't get to it?"

Bank business concluded, they head down the road to the Chrystal Hill VA clinic, park, and head inside. Frankie shows his new identification card. The admissions clerk opens the file and reads a note, perks right up. "Yes, sir, Captain Cooper. Doctor Beans will be right with you. You're in good hands here, don't worry."

A little more courteous than the admissions desk at the last clinic earlier in the week, the clerk punches a button on the desktop. "Mary Anne, Captain Cooper's here for Doctor Beans."

Frankie asks about his claim and back pay. The clerk says, "Tennessee had the field records. Your files arrived last night by currier from several clinics, a bit unusual but we have it all. You never filed here in the Chicago district, always elsewhere, so no one clinic had everything, only Tennessee has your discharge and medical files. You never went back. VA won't go looking. The veterans have to come in. We can't go find you. Why would we? How could we?"

"So," Frankie says, "I get a check now?"

"Yeah, we always pay it, once it's approved, retroactive from the date of claim. Just gotta come in, fill out all the papers, prove it, and get the doctors certificates. Takes awhile, only a month or so usually because your original claim was approved over two years ago. Probably take us a month to process it now that we have the back records."

Frankie says, "A month? You said you have all the records. Why so long?"

"Takes time, we need to verify the documents."

Jake butts in, a little grit in his voice. "Take more time? Why? To do it all again? Been done at least once and approved ... Can I get your full name, and number here?"

"Evan Morales," he says. "I just do what VA tells me. I can't change it, or hurry it." Morales chuckles briefly, "I'm just a peon admissions clerk." Morales offers a card.

A tall, thin nurse with short silver hair pushes open a door. "Frank Cooper?" Frankie pops up a hand. "Come with me, please. Doctor Beans will see you now." She arches her eyebrows as Jake follows Frankie into the room, but says nothing.

"Sam Beans, Medical Director here," he says, offering a hand. "Miller's a good friend. We go all the way back to Boston College together. Played basketball. Didn't win a lot, but had fun, drank a few beers, chased a little tail, and got an education. He says good things about both of you. Thanks for what you did for us, and our country."

Both Jake and Frankie shake his hand and nod at the compliment. "You too, doc. You were right there with us, keeping us alive. Different times, same battles."

"Let's take a look at that stump. We have your new prosthetic coming in tomorrow." He grins. "Apparently we both know a certain Senator that spreads some pretty heavy juice around."

The doctor completes a thorough exam, looks over the same x-rays Tuttle took that also magically arrived overnight, and makes the same remarks.

Good surgeon. Stump's just a little beat up from the wrong fittings."

"From everything in your record, and what you both tell me today, I'd like you to stay here with us for a couple weeks. We need to fit the new foot correctly, teach a little PT, learn balance, and I want to do some psyche evaluations, maybe heal your mind a bit. Best to do it here, not by outpatient appointment. It'll be quicker, and you'll stay here where we can find you, not traipsing around the country. We'll try a couple meds that stabilize your brain chemistry. We'll figure it out, Coop, if you give us a little time."

"Captain Cooper won't like that much, Jake." Frankie squirms in his seat. "Nothing wrong with my mind. I like it just fine the way it is, like my new tent, too."

A clinic bed holds no appeal for this vagrant. Frankie likes the outdoors, always has, even as a youngster. He reaches into his pocket, wraps his fingers around the handkerchief and strokes his carved oak face.

Jake puts a hand on his shoulder, "You need this Coop. Let yourself heal."

Frankie thinks it over, rubs the oak stub for a minute longer. A little security and comfort soaks into his fist, calms the stress. He glances back and forth between Jake and the doctor. "Okay. Captain says it's okay."

Sam Beans tells Jake, "I'll take good care, and call you if anything comes up. You're in good hands here, Coop."

Frankie bends forward. "Let me see your hands." Sam Beans shows his hands, palms up. Frankie takes a look, examines each one. "Everyone I meet here tells me I'm in really good hands, so I want to see what good hands look like."

"I'm heading west today or tomorrow, Coop. Miss my wife and kids, and have been on the road over a month this time." He hands Sam Beans a card. "You can reach me at this number twenty-four, seven. Please keep it private, between us."

Frankie hugs Jake. More than a minute passes. "You take care Jake, tell Sarah hello for me, and Jimmy Dodds too, if you see him."

Jake leaves Frankie with the doctor and steps out into the lobby, pulls out his phone and dials. "Winston here. What's up Jake?" His voice crackles over the line.

"Got a name and a number. Evan Morales, here at the VA clinic tells us Coop has his pension papers all approved two years ago but wants another month to verify and release payment. Coop deserves better than another delay."

"VA benefits, it's not free medical care, like some folks believe. He earned it Miller, like every other veteran that puts his life on the line. Frankie bought his with a foot. Some soldiers pay more."

"I've got the clinic number right here, I'll rattle a chain in a minute. Got some info on the dead cell you asked about, too."

The senator explains in general how wireless phone technology works, then how a techie might tweak it so it sounds like a dead-end.

"Once the guy, probably Porter, hacked that connection, he set up a phone relay through the local tower. That's why no one there traced it. After they killed the handsets, the relay hits the tower and bounces back to the same cell, and never left that tower. It was like dialing himself each time."

"Pretty slick actually and unless the home office knew exactly where to look, they wouldn't, it's too simple. So, the sheriff got nothing with a standard trace, just a dead line. Multiple cell numbers act like the same phone dialing itself. The caller never hears anything but an empty line. And, it's not recordable."

"But if the caller speaks or punches any two button sequence, the phone link hits a live recorder and the recipient just plugs in and listens when he gets back. If a caller knows the process, caller leaves a message. If caller doesn't know, it sounds like a dead phone and the caller hangs up. Apparently, these guys told the clients to hit number one and two when they called, so it kicked on the recorder. Anyone randomly calling in got silence."

Jake pulls out a small notebook and listens, writes down some names and numbers, an address. "Most of this is already a dead end Jake, but if you can put it together with what that deputy knows, might find the guy you want. Take care of yourself and Coop, and keep in touch." The phone clicks off.

Five seconds later the admissions phone chirps. Evan Morales picks up, "Chrystal Hill VA clinic, Morales." The clerk straightens up as sharp words come over the line. Nearly sitting at attention by the time a string of orders runs out, he says, "Yes sir, Senator. Will take care of it. One week, yes sir, in his bank account or my head will roll." Morales hangs up, jumps out of his seat and quick-steps down the hall into the financial affairs office.

Jake heads back into the clinic, finds Frankie sitting on a bed in a single room staring at a handkerchief. Frankie slips the red rag in his pocket as Jake steps in through the door.

He shares all the information Miller Winston told him. Tells Frankie to give it all to Deputy Joe, and Tick, and Ellie, and keep that investigator in the loop too. "Scott Monroe seems pretty sharp, Coop, let him help," Jake says. "You know who and where, it's up to you all and Deputy Joe to handle these guys now."

"I'm out of here on a red-eye tonight. Deputy Joe seems like a good cop. He'll figure it out, but I can't stay any longer. This may be all I'll get even if I stay. It's in the right place, Coop, the sheriff's office. The feds will step in if this bank fraud falls out on the table anyway. You know how to reach me if you need me. Just keep me informed."

Jake hops in the Buick and aims it at the airport. Four hours later he's in the air, flying west at over six hundred miles an hour. Next stop, Los Angeles.

Chapter Sixteen

Scott picks up Tick and Ellie on random days and evenings and follows the man they know as Cliff Porter each time he departs the office. At the moment, all three sit in the Blazer across the street in a market storefront parking lot, watching the complex.

One guy drives a BMW and seems to be the boss, probably the man Ellie says calls himself Mitchell, and another guy Scott says is John Reardon works with these two as well. All three occasionally hang out at a club called EATS 'n DRINKS, a combination bar and restaurant where boss man seems to spend a lot more time than the other two.

Scott says, "The place serves pretty good food, and it's not a chain. I stop in whenever my work takes me over into this county. I've been in enough it's no big deal. Next time one of them heads over to EATS, I'll go in and order a sandwich, see what happens."

"Ten days," Tick says, "and we got nothing concrete. Seems the gang is three guys, with one security guard during the day. Two addresses where this John guy appears to meet with two couples at home, senior clients maybe, and that club where all three hang out. We can't know for sure if the couples are clients or friends, or what."

Ellie says, "John's probably running the same seniors game on these folks. Wish there was a way to know for certain without asking. If these are just friends or relatives, we tip our hand if we ask."

No luck gathering evidence and no plan to change that emerges. Ellie believes Cliff might recognize her since she met him twice at her grandparent's home. "He stared at me like I was a piece of pie. Very creepy dude."

She never met John in person, but John dealt with Gina and Mickey McGee most of the time, whenever he brought papers to sign and collect the investment funds. Ellie was usually absent when either one of the two arrived, either working or attending her college classes.

* * *

Monday morning on his way out to pick up Tick and Ellie, Scott drives past the offices and discovers the building empty. "Damn, we should have taken shifts, watched them closer."

Scott blames himself. He feels a little anger rise up at his own stupidity. He's no amateur and should have known. He continues down the county blacktop and turns south on the highway toward the encampment, ready to share the unfortunate news.

Scott pulls into the gravel turnout, Tick and Ellie climb in, he tells about the vacant building. "Well, at least we know where they hang out, we can watch EATS and pick one up there and follow him again."

Tick says, "I'm beginning to feel a bit like Sam Spade or Colombo, maybe even good old Sherlock Holmes."

* * *

Back at the VA clinic, Sam Beans dials a number on the card Jake left. The phone clicks twice and a relay routes it. It rings once. A live person answers. "Tango Detail, code please."

"I don't have a code. I need to speak with Jacoby Klyne. Doctor Sam Beans here."

"No one here by that name."

"Can I leave a message?"

"No one here by that name."

"Okay. If you ever meet him, tell him Doctor Samuel Beans called, and Frank Cooper left two days ago without checking out." He glances at the phone face and finds the line disconnected. He double checks the number he dialed, shrugs, sets the phone down and begins reviewing his clinic notes. A few minutes pass. His phone chirps once, he flips it open. "Doctor Beans."

The familiar female voice says, "Tango Detail. Jacoby Klyne is out of state on assignment. He received your message." The phone disconnects again. Beans stares at the phone face a few seconds and grins. "Weird, must be a spy."

Chapter Seventeen

Deputy Joe pulls on a hair cap and a pair of rubber gloves, points at the autopsy table. "What's your take on it, Jack?"

"Caucasian male, six foot one, thin, only a hundred seventy pounds, black hair, probably late forties, and a smoker." The medical investigator hovers over a body laid out on a steel tray, several dissection cuts run down the chest. The investigator rolls what remains of Cliff up on his side and peels the skin back, uncovers the spinal column at the back of his neck.

"Neck broke before he hit the river," the investigator says. "He didn't drown. No water in his lungs. Broken neck killed him. Could've done it when the Acura flipped off the bridge. We'll have to wait for the on-scene report but it looks a little odd, the cervical axis twisted and snapped, crushed the nerve bundle. A little unusual to see it in a car rollover like this one."

"So, an accident, or no?" Deputy Joe asks.

"Won't discount an accident, can't call it anything else at this point until we get the lab work and the field report."

"And someone removed the maintenance gate before the car went off the bridge," the coroner adds. "That could be anything. Kids sneak down by the river and screw or smoke pot, and that gate's been removed numerous times in the past. They just cut the lock and push it over. Hunters too, taking four wheelers into the woods along the river. So, it ain't unusual for that gate to be down. That's two oddities in this one, but not enough to raise any alarm with the cops or the ADA. Or me. Looks like he slid off the bank in the snow. Rental car in the name of Richard Everett outta Idaho."

"But, an interesting fact," Deputy Joe says, "We ran his fingerprints and found a criminal record. That conviction shows financial crimes in Seattle under the name Daryl Montgomery, not Cliff Patterson as this false driver's license shows. We believe he may be the same Cliff Porter that hired Tank and his cronies. He fits the description exactly."

"Give me a head shot, Jack, maybe I'll go find out."

The coroner slips an eight by ten face-on and a profile photograph into a large manila envelope, tells Joe, "Keep it."

* * *

Deputy Joe keys the gate leading into the holding cells. "All right, Tank and you two goons in training, take a look at these."

He holds up two photos. "Is this the guy?"

Tank wastes three seconds of his life and asks a stupid question. "Do we get off if we help you ID this guy, Joe?"

"Nope. But I'll give you an extra dessert tonight and we won't kick your ass after lights out if you identify him." Joe laughs. "Just kidding, Tank. You're already beat up enough, and the court's gonna kick it anyway, if not Maggie sure will if she gits to you first."

Pretty open and shut case with the confessions, and knife wound on Tank's cheek and a cut hand. Joe's not worried, but he'd like an ID if it's Porter.

Tank says, "Okay, we'll take chocolate cake. That's the guy." All three agree.

Deputy Joe just shakes his head and walks away, grinning. "Idiots."

Chapter Eighteen

The vagabond clan wakes up and spots a classic GMC four-wheel drive pickup parked up along the gravel turn-out painted the original color, two-tone blue and white. Suddenly, Frankie appears from the south, jogging north on the highway with a rhythmic running gait, no limp. He's wearing clean, pressed fatigues and light gray Nikes. He grabs his coat out of the truck, drops down the slope toward the camp, slips and falls, bounces up laughing like the athlete he once was earlier in his life, and has again become.

Annie offers Frankie a cup of her morning brew, a shot of Jack Daniel's in it helps ease the chill. He joins Ellie and Tick at the burn barrel, explains the new foot, how well it fits and lets him walk normal and even run again.

"Awesome," he says, "So comfortable I almost don't know it's there. Doc said I fought the misfit foot so long it built calluses, and I kept up the PT. The muscles stayed fit and strong. Balance training went much quicker than usual. Didn't really need PT."

Frankie wanders over to the culvert, finds Junkie hiding on his bunk sewing a rip in his shirt. "No laughing allowed," Junkie points a smile at him and Frankie laughs anyway.

"Hey, need you to take a peek at this pickup. Just bought it, a sixty-eight with a two-eighty-three, Junkie. The old guy bought it brand new, but his eyes got nerve damage or something and he can't see to drive it anymore. State took his license. Truck cost five grand. Seems to run fine and look fine, but if it needs something, the Captain would like to know."

Junkie glances over at the oak tree and back at Frankie. "Good price. What, some crazy relative die and make you rich?"

"Nope, the VA finally paid off for my foot. Jake helped get the papers right. Captain Cooper could've come along and helped if he'd a mind to but he's kinda rooted to that spot over there." Frankie giggles at his own joke. Junkie laughs with him.

"Okay. Junkie 'the friend' will take a free peek. Junkie 'the mechanic' will fix it for a small fee plus parts if it needs fixing. We'll take it down to the horse barn later, get us outta this cold and snow. Tell the Captain it sounds pretty good from here. Heard it when you drove up earlier. Sure looks clean, the owner really took good care of it."

"Yup, not a ding in it and no rust," Frankie says. "Fair's fair. I can clean out a stall or two for Arnold and Sue, too. A little trade for some dry work space." Junkie and Frankie bump fists, a done deal.

Deputy Joe eases in off the highway, works his way down the slope. "Ellie around?" Ellie crawls out of the alcove Shanty abandoned where she and Tick now sleep and store the gear.

"Seems like that guy you been tracking for the fraud case wound up dead two days ago. His Acura flipped off the bridge and landed upside down in the river, car flooded with the driver still in it. No seat belt. Broke his neck. Thought maybe you should know about it." He explains the coroner's findings, the fake name and the Seattle criminal record. "A little odd but Jack's not taking it any farther, labeled it an accident."

Frankie asks, "So, that's it? Closed case. No investigation?"

"Well, an accident with conditions, he told us. He leaves it open for ninety days. Unless something new tells him different it'll probably close out as a DUI incident. Looks pretty much like it is though. Guy had some alcohol in his blood, not a lot, and the rest of it's just speculation. We told the FBI but Hargrove ignored it, as usual."

"We pushed two photos at Tank and his goons," Deputy Joe continues. "All three said the same thing. Cliff Porter. Pretty interesting, ain't it?"

The fingerprints point us at the criminal record in Seattle and the real name, Daryl Montgomery. Fraud conviction fits, guess he ain't changed his spots, just his name."

Tick reminds Joe, "Ellie told Hargrove more than once that those farm boys assaulting Heath was part of a financial fraud case. She says he doesn't believe her,"

"Mister 'full-of-himself' Hargrove's still jacking off about us beating up the thug triplets as retaliation for the attack on Heath, too. He needs a life, preferably in another district, like maybe Alaska or even Siberia would be excellent," Joe concludes.

"I'll send the FBI a copy. Can't give you one, but I'll let you read it. Putting all this together, the photos and the investigator report, and the odd autopsy, might be you and Ellie can get Brenda Davis to look at it. Get rid of that lazy fool Hargrove. Maybe I'll route it directly to Davis instead, include my opinion. Then you two go chat with her. FBI won't do anything about the beating, no jurisdiction, but if it ties in with mortgage fraud, then you'll get their support facilities looking at all of it."

Deputy Joe climbs the embankment and heads out to prepare his report and Fax a copy over to Brenda Davis, the new FBI District Supervisor.

Ellie and Tick dust the snow off a log and grab a seat by the burn barrel. Ellie says, "That friend of Frankie, Jake Klyne seems a bit secretive. I think he knows some things we don't."

"Both seem very fit, if it weren't for Jake's light hair it'd be hard to tell them apart in the dark. Same size, same athletic build, and those same inquisitive eyes. Look right through you, like analyzing the situation constantly. I'd hate to tangle with either one in a dark alley, even Frankie with only one foot."

Tick continues, "I'm thinking maybe Jake beat up those thugs too, but have no clue how he found them if he did. Suddenly, all three go in all beat to hell, and confess. That story, 'truck hit a fence', doesn't hold water with me or with Deputy Joe either. Someone forced those guys into giving themselves up."

"They both served together too, but Frankie won't talk about it much. Just that he lost his foot in Panama. Frankie told us Jake carried him out, saved his life," Ellie says.

Tick rubs his head, trying to fit the puzzle together in his mind. "Just seems a little fishy to me, but in a good way for us. Jake shows up, helps Frankie with the VA mess. The triplets get beat up and confess out of nowhere, and then Cliff Porter or Patterson, whoever he is, ends up in the river under less than ordinary conditions. And exactly on the weekend these guys move out of their offices, one ends up dead in the water. And, has served time for financial fraud. Seems a bit weird, too coincidental."

"One more interesting thing, Jake takes Frankie to the clinic, and we don't see either one for almost two weeks. Jake told us he was heading to Los Angeles and Frankie to the VA clinic. But both are gone when this car accident happens."

Ellie adds, "Why would Jake help us, and Heath? He doesn't even know us."

"Frankie and Heath became friends pretty quickly, both military. Maybe Frankie felt an obligation and asked Jake to help."

"Right, but that means we have to assume Jake actually came all this way on a whim and did all that, including beating three guys he doesn't even know and killing a guy, and with no real evidence Jake did anything at all," Ellie says. "Then he disappears. Confusing, for sure and pretty hard to believe. Extremely hard to believe, actually."

"Makes no sense to me," Tick says. "That accident could easily have been just an accident in slick snow or ice on that curve. Wrecks happen often in weather like this."

Tick drops his head down onto his palms, rubs his temples. "We could be reading a lot into this too. Convenient for us, pick and choose answers that fit, ignore things that don't."

"Right, and then Frankie shows up, back from the clinic with a new foot and a pick-up truck. How weird is that, when you drop that and all the rest into the mix."

"Okay, the crooks moved, as if they knew someone was watching," Tick says, "Maybe the FBI scared 'em. We don't know. But we at least know the club where one hangs out. We can stake out EATS and pick him up again if he ever goes back."

"Damn, that's a lot of hours outside that club. Wish we had an FBI team. We should do what Joe suggested, check in with the supervisor."

"Don't know, Tick. Sounds a little thin to me and we want it more than anyone else at this point. Will sound even thinner to the FBI. Won't hurt to ask Agent

Davis though. She can only say no. Be better if we had more evidence."

Chapter Nineteen

John Randle pulls into the parking lot, heads into the office. "Harold, have you seen Cliff? Has he called in? He's not answering."

"Nope, nothing since two days ago. He didn't show yesterday at all, or call in. Mister Emory asked the same thing. He's inside, and pissed. Cliff ain't answering his cell or a text or a page."

John pushes into the main office. "Where's Cliff?"

Emory shakes his head. "No clue. He was supposed to bring those signatures back yesterday and the final mortgage check from Ingles."

Harold hurries into the office two minutes behind John. "Look at this! Just opened the newspaper and found it." Harold shows both men a photo on the front page. An Acura lies upside down in the river, the water level nearly up to its wheels. A tow truck cable stretched tight and hooked to an axle appears to be reeling the Acura out of the river. Below that headline photo, a reprint from an Idaho license shows a head shot of Cliff.

The headline reads: Man found dead in a flip-over on Old River Road.

All three read the lead story explaining the Acura seemingly missed a curve on the icy road and flipped into the river, killing the driver the night before last. A falsified Idaho driver's in the name of Cliff Patterson was found in the victim's wallet, along with credit cards in the same name.

Sheriff's department said the man was not wearing a seat belt and alcohol may be a factor. The incident remains under investigation by the coroner's office while they search for the true identity of a white male driver approximately forty-five years of age. A statement at the end asks if anyone recognizes the man in this photo please call Deputy Joe Eagleton at the county offices.

"No wonder he didn't show yesterday!" Emory barks. The pages fly apart as he throws the paper across the room. "Dumb fuck, this really screws things up! Why now? Just when we're ready to wrap up this set and take a break!"

"Least that ID tracks back to Idaho. Won't give us any trouble here," John says.

Emory rubs his jaw, thinking this new development through. "Let's clear out anything with his name on it, and burn it. John, you head over to his rooms and get rid if anything there as well. That Acura's a lease to the Richard Everett ID and Idaho license. Nothing there connecting to us either. Cops have a mess on their hands trying to connect Cliff with Everett too. It goes nowhere. None of those people are real, there's no history connecting anyone to them or to us."

"Yeah. Fine, that's a dead end. All right, let's put an ad in the local paper. See if we can hire another salesman with no morals or ethics." Emory laughs out loud and kicks a chair across the room. "Should be a dime a dozen."

Neither John nor Harold finds humor in his sarcasm. Harold ducks his head, slips out into the corridor and returns to his kiosk as if he feels guilty for bringing in the bad news.

John butts in. "It's an accident. Coroner will probably rule it a DUI as we were down at EATS drinking earlier that night, right before it happened. Cliff stayed when I left. Sheriff will probably drop it. Maybe we can follow it up without looking too interested. It shouldn't bother us. We only got two deals running now anyway."

"All right, John. Where do we stand with his contacts?"

"Don't know, will check his notes before we burn it all. Only know one that may become a problem. Alexandria. She's upset and backing out, and her daughter knows. She's that attorney in San Francisco. And, Cliff was supposed to bring back the Ingles check. Might be a problem if the sheriff finds it."

"Well, if anything hits back at us, we can try to blame it all on Cliff," Emory says. "He has a record for fraud, we can rat on him. If they show up, tell the cops we didn't know what he was doing with these folks."

Randle adds, "Guess we better hold everything up a week or two until we can figure out where to take this."

"How many names do we have ready in the mill?"

Cliff was running these two, Ingles and Alexandria," Randle says, "I can meet with Ingles, but he told Alexandria you fired me when she got upset. We promised her money back this week, and we put her off one extra week already. You'll have to settle that one yourself. We have three new contacts sitting in the trough waiting to start. That's it. Then we're done unless we can find a way to search more names. I have no clue how to run that program Cliff wrote."

"Have we run the family background on those yet?"

"Not sure, that was Cliff, too. Will check his notes and see where we sit with anyone currently in the files."

"Okay. I'm outta here," Emory says. "Going down to EATS and get a drink, try to figure something out."

* * *

Carlton Emory enters EATS, sits at the end of the bar atop his regular stool. The bartender greets him. "Hey Cal." Sets a napkin and a scotch rocks on the bar without asking.

Emory sips, glances around the room, discovers it less than half full, the after work crowd still working, the lunch crowd gone already. "Hey Gordy, gimme a ham and Swiss, some of those famous spicy fries, and a draft to chase it." Emory eyeballs a petite, dark-haired, attractive woman dressed in blue jeans, boots, and a bright red blouse sitting alone at the bar, nursing a drink. "Who's the gal?" Both men turn and look briefly, admiring.

"Patty Pearson, Jimmy's ex-wife as of a couple months ago. She comes in now and again, a local farm girl born and raised right here. Jimmy Pearson's the district supervisor."

"Bring her a drink, Gordy."

"Ain't your type, Cal. She'll chew you up and spit you out without even breathing hard."

"Fix whatever she's drinking." Gordy sets a glass on the bar, drops ice and pours, adds a little water. Emory holds up five fingers. Gordy pops a thumb up, and nods.

Emory picks up her drink and his own. He struts over toward the woman like an alpha dog sniffing the scent and sets the tumbler on the bar beside her. He offers his hand, flashes his teeth, and says a few words. Patty Pearson ignores him.

He says a few more words, puts a little more hustle in it. She turns, smiles and leans in close, lays a hand on his knee, flexes the muscle in her forearm. Emory squirms in his seat, a twinge crosses his face, and he grunts. She whispers two distinct words in his ear then slides the drink he bought into the bar tray and turns her face toward the mirror as if he's invisible.

Emory shrugs, leaves his empty glass sitting on the bar, grabs her drink off the tray, and returns to his seat just as his sandwich and fries arrive. "Fuck her." Emory slaps a five dollar bill on the bar and rubs his knee, feeling more pain in it than he imagined possible from a woman that small. He downs half the drink he bought for Patty Pearson.

Gordy collects the bet, and slips the fiver in his shirt pocket, sets a draft next to the plate, adds a napkin wrapped around a knife and a fork, and grins. "Told ya'."

* * *

Emory sits at his desk across from his one remaining partner. "Interesting dilemma we find ourselves in, John. We just increased our net worth by thirty-three percent."

John responds with a puzzled look. "How's that?"

"Good old Cliff drank himself into that river, and no one has access to our offshore accounts but you and me now." No Cheshire cat ever showed a wider grin than the one crossing Emory's face.

Suddenly, John gets it too and grins just as wide. "Ha. Never thought of that."

"Maybe we ought to wrap up this investment business and go legit," Emory says. "No worry about the Feds, no worry about hiding the money. We can relax, take a trip. Find a couple gals that don't care about commitment, just fun."

"Probably have to pay 'em," John offers.

"So what? We can afford it. Pay for it, it comes without sniveling."

Both men sit reflecting for a moment, contemplating the future. Emory breaks the silence. "Maybe we should give back the Alexandria funds. She's gonna push that attorney daughter at us pretty hard. She lied about holding the complaint and already filed it. We got nothing else on the board that can hit us that hard."

"Legitimate business!" Emory ponders that thought a moment. "Ha ... never thought I'd attach that label to myself."

"Yeah, me neither."

"Well John, might be a nice change. We can always move to a new location again, go back to this if we don't like it."

Chapter Twenty

Back at the hobo camp, the remaining residents pack in for the night. Snow falls heavily and carries a brittle freeze in with it. Annie climbs up into Junkie's bunk, alone, and wraps herself in tight. Junkie caught a couple free nights and meals at Sue and Arnold's barn in exchange for repairing a plow truck, a typical deal Junkie finagles when the snow comes in hard. Frankie lies snug and comfortable in his new tent beneath the watchful eyes of his Captain Cooper tree.

Ellie and Tick crawl into the cave-like hollow Shanty abandoned when he took off for North Carolina. The pair figures they own it at least until they leave for warmer weather, or Shanty returns in the spring. The pint-sized bush cave leaves things a bit crowded for two, and they've not yet made a transition to a couple, or even discussed or acted upon that possibility. The loss of his brother and her lover makes that taboo for now. The memory of Heath hovers above the relationship like a spirit floating on the breeze and not yet acknowledged by either one.

Ellie and Tick each slide down inside a sleeping bag laid out atop a thick ground pad. Ellie glances at Tick and catches him watching her again. A serene but somewhat uncomfortable emotion permeates the tight space, neither one willing to attempt a new liaison at the moment with the loss of Heath still raw in both minds.

Her relationship with Heath was more casual in her than with Heath. Heath felt a much stronger emotional pull between them, and voiced it a few times. Ellie responded more as a companion than a true lover, and treated Heath as convenience and comfort between two travelers, nothing permanent. Heath accepted it and enjoyed it for what it was, and had hoped the time they spent together might change her mind.

Now Ellie puzzles over the bond she feels between two brothers, one a memory now, and the other real and alive. The two so alike physically but so different emotionally and mentally and what that means to her in the life she now leads. Her entire purpose at the moment aims at the revelation and punishment of the men who stole the retirement money from her family, and sent the thug triplets to beat Heath.

In that regard, Tick feels identically vengeful. He's already voiced many times that he won't leave this area until his brother finds peace, and believes Heath won't find peace until those responsible parties receive justice and a proper penalty.

Ellie says, "What can we do about these fraudsters? Deputy Joe isn't getting anywhere, and the FBI ignores it as if it didn't happen. Joe's happy enough to arrest the thugs and prosecute the murder. His job's mainly finished. The man that hired them died in the river, an accident. Joe accepts that. Where else can he go with it?"

"Two different things, Ellie, but the same crooks did it," Tick says. "But both police organizations treat it as different and separate events. One's a beating, an assault, now a murder, a state crime. The other a bank fraud, a federal crime. Probably get better results if law enforcement agencies worked together and compared notes."

"Yeah, well, no one believes the connection, and that two crooks are still out there, planning and ripping off more victims like my grandparents."

"And the biggest surprise," Tick says, "Scott told me yesterday they refunded Virginia Alexandria's investment, complete with interest. That buries the only link we have now, and after that refund, the FBI believes we're nuts to accuse these two men of fraud."

"So, it's not gonna happen officially, it seems. Maybe we should make a plan and get even ourselves. We don't need any more evidence, that's for sure." Ellie fluffs two large bath towels beneath her head and shut her eyes. "Maybe if we sleep on it, we'll come up with something."

Tick stares at her for a few moments, watching her slip into sleep, appreciating her as a woman, a companion, but still a possession that belongs to his brother at least in spirit. He rolls up his coat, slides it under his head, and drifts off into oblivion.

Snow falls continuously for several hours. Two bodies feel the cold seep into the hut. Each one struggles with the chill and slips a little closer. Tick awakens and discovers Ellie sleeping tight against his back, her left arm draped across his shoulder. He turns toward Ellie and lays a hand lightly on her hip but outside the fabric of her sleeping bag. He holds himself in check, allowing Ellie the response she chooses.

Abruptly, Ellie awakens and feels the closeness. She locks eyes with Tick a few seconds until a tear builds in the corner of each eye then removes her arm, slides sideways and rolls onto her back, fluffing up her towels again and aiming her gaze at the interwoven sticks and patchy canvas ceiling. A single tear dribbles down each cheek.

The narrow space between them spreads into an imaginary gorge a mile deep and a mile wide, defeating both touch and conversation. Ellie snuggles deeper into her bag and shuts her eyes again. Puzzled and pondering, Tick watches her sleep, enjoying the comfort and fighting the chill, until his eyes slide shut and sleep captures him again.

Chapter Twenty-one

Wrapped in a heavy coat, wearing a fur hat with ear flaps and old rubber milking boots, Annie kicks her way through the snow, and pumps propane into an aged Coleman stove. The odor of fresh coffee fills the air just as daylight breaks and begins glistening off a few snowflakes still swirling lightly about the encampment.

Frankie pushes out of his tent, knocks the snow off it, and grabs his cup, "Don't know how you do it Annie, you always wake up before dawn."

"Had to feed chickens and goats every day while growing up, gather eggs and milk or we didn't eat. That kinda stays with you all your life. Besides, I love watching the sun come up when the day ain't had time to beat you down yet."

Tick and Ellie stomp a path over to the burn barrel, start feeding more fuel into the fire and watch the blaze flare up into the dawn. Both dust the snow off a log and sit.

"We gotta make a plan, figure out some way to get back at these guys. FBI cares less what we think, and Deputy Joe got his man, or men, or punks, whichever. None of those law enforcement guys believe what we know for certain," Ellie says. "No way am I giving up now that we're sure who did it."

Frankie slips a bottle out of his coat, unscrews the cap and takes a pull. "Captain thinks you should get them same way they get everyone else. Figure out a scheme, and scam them back." All four stare across the fire at one another, no one responds. Frankie shrugs. "Why not? Works for them, can work for us too." Frankie caps the pint, tosses the bottle over to Annie.

Annie pours a shot into her coffee and passes it on. "This'll get our brains warmed up and working." She drags up a grin."Got another one under the culvert when this runs out. Junkie hid it, but I know his secret stash." She cuts loose a short girlish giggle like only Annie can and it squeals up into the dawn. Just as it happens each time she lets it loose, all four break into laughter, a contagious activity no sane person can resist.

"We'll pay him back ... besides, he's nice and warm in the loft, and probably sipping apple wine with Arnold. Serves 'em both right to miss out on this pint, staying up in the barn with all those critters." Annie pinches the tip of her nose and giggles again. "Course, that has its own personal penalties."

Frankie glances at his tree "Last night Captain told me, 'we ain't dumb, just homeless'. Right Captain? So, let's figure it out." He slips his hand in this pocket, rubs his mobile stub face, draws out a little comfort but keeps his idol private, hiding it even from his friends.

Snow chains rattle on the icy highway. A pickup truck rumbles in and idles above the culvert. Junkie climbs out and slips and slides his way down the slope and joins the group, rubs his hands together over the flames.

"Got tired of that stink," he says. "Couple horses and cows staying inside for the storm squeezed all the fresh air outta that barn in a hurry, even the sleeping loft. Barney pushed his way in, too. Damn billy-goat smells worse than Gator. That ended my visit."

Annie slides over and makes room. "You be the one trespassing, Junkie. That's home to those critters." She hands Junkie what remains of his hidden bottle, and grins.

"Thanks for saving me at least a sip," he says, and tips it up while Annie recounts the morning, bringing Junkie up to date on the retribution idea.

Ellie says, "I know what they did to my grandparents. How can that help us?"

"Can you get the papers? We can get some ideas from it," Frankie asks.

"Yup, Granny copied everything for that attorney she hired that did nothing for us except cash his checks. I carry it around in my backpack, just in case." She ducks into the cubby and hauls out a manila envelope containing the fraudulent paperwork, starts sharing it page by page, passing it around so everyone gets a peek at the real thing.

For the rest of the day, a light snow drifts and swirls around the camp, but the fire and the collusion keeps everyone engaged in plotting revenge. One plan, they reject, then another, then another. Collective brainpower fits one piece of a plan with one piece of another, like a jigsaw puzzle, and by the end of the day several ideas begin making sense, and a devious and ingenious plot emerges.

The mood improves despite the weather, and the more they talk, the bolder they become. Annie jumps up, starts dancing in a circle, pumps a fist in the air, slips and falls in a pile of snow, squealing the whole time. "That'll work, Ellie, that'll work. Ha, we got 'em. Kick those bastards right in the wallet." She dusts herself off and staggers, falls again, laughing the while time, feeling that spike she laced in her coffee all day.

"Captain Cooper says kick 'em somewhere else while we're at it."

"Well, there too," Annie agrees, and everyone shares another laugh.

"Okay, okay, maybe," Tick says. "But we need money to get this started. Then it'll feed itself if it works." The thought pulls the joy down a notch. The group ponders that new dilemma until the fire dims and the cold ripples in, breaking up the party.

"You mean, when it works," Ellie corrects Tick.

"Money." Annie offers the first installment. "I got two grand in the bank, savings from farms jobs I picked up during harvest and canning season. Will put up half, as long as the plan works and it comes back to me."

Ellie says, "It'll work, one way or the other. I've got three grand savings from the last tax season. And, got that temporary job for the CPA again this year in a couple months. So can put it back then."

"Anyone puts money up gets back double when we collect, after we pay back my grandparents, anything left we divide according to the amount and effort we each put up."

Junkie offers next, "I got a grand, half my nut. That's about it for me 'til after the spring when I git all the local plant and fertilizer gear up and running again."

"Our mother willed us a small trust, put her life savings in and bought an insurance policy on me, and Heath, and our sister. Cassandra lives in Boston and maintains it. The trust also pays out a few hundred bucks a month to each of us. We just call her and she sends it when we need it."

Ellie butts in. "Yeah, Heath always had a few bucks in his pocket, even when he didn't find any day-labor. Wondered about it but he never said. That explains it."

"I'll call my sister tomorrow. Bet she'll give me her half of the insurance on Heath to help find out who set this all up. Each policy's worth ten thousand, we split it. We're the only family left now. And we know this goes beyond Cliff."

Ellie easily adds the figures. "Well, that's fifteen grand in total. We'll try to make that work. We will make that work." She corrects herself, confident she can pull it off. Her role, seducing Emory without actually seducing him. Run a scam and retrieve the fraud funds from his bank accounts.

The barrel burns low, the chill creeps in, and the thoughts turn inward as each member contemplates a part in the retribution scheme. Ellie pushes up and heads off toward the cubby. Tick follows in her footsteps. Frankie hauls himself over and confers with his oak tree for a minute or two, salutes, and crawls into his tent.

"Come on, Junkie, gittin' cold out here. Got a nice buzz on and feel a bit frisky tonight." A little unsteady on her feet, Annie aims her nose toward the culvert, her girlish giggle echoing into the forest. Junkie pops up like a jack-in-the-box that suddenly grew feet and tags right along behind her, a big old grin lighting up his face.

Chapter Twenty-two

Carlton Emory and John Randle lean up against the bar inside EATS and discuss the future, deciding whether they should transfer the operation and most of the cash into a legitimate firm, get a legal license, and build a real estate empire.

Grand delusions fill the conversation. Both men believe they sit at the top of the heap in any endeavor they attempt, and believe they can achieve any goal they set. Neither man lacks for selfishness or ego. Both think the world owes them a living.

"Superb planning, that's what breeds success," Emory claims, "and that we have." His words slur a bit, reflecting his early arrival at the bar today. A bubble of drool runs down his chin.

"Keep 'em coming Gordy, we're celebrating our new company, Green Pastures Real Estate and Development, specializing in mid-level retirement homes for senior golfers." Emory winks at Randle, and whispers, "And no more thirty percent fee to Bennett for cleaning our money. He's worse than fuckin' IRS." Both men laugh aloud, after deciding this morning the color of that illustrious green paper they both crave must somehow embed itself in the company name.

Cliff left only three names on his hustle list, and he was the senior finder, so Emory needs another crooked tech expert. Or, he might just finish these three and retire for a few years, find a tech, then resume the scam in another location, a different state.

Together, Emory and Randle decided earlier in the day they might launch a legal real estate firm and see where it takes them. Neither one understands technology well enough to continue this scam. Cliff brought special talents to the table, including a new website that provided an old and proven track record complete with four and five star reviews each time the scammers moved and changed names.

Both men understand how difficult it would be to find another tech specialist trustworthy enough to provide the tech work necessary for the background clients see when they review the company, and also mingle with clients and suck them into the fraud-based operation they've been running together for several years.

Randle glances at Emory and tips up his glass, offering a toast, "Thanks Cliff, for your perfectly timed swim in the river. Left us high and dry for a tech expert, but increased our bank account." The smaller partner of the two, John Randle matches Emory drink for drink all afternoon, and he slurs his words even worse than Emory. Both men clink glasses and empty the remaining scotch in one long swallow.

"One more." Emory holds up two fingers, contradicting himself. Gordy ignores the singular order, and sets two scotch and water with ice on the napkins almost before the words leave Emory's mouth.

Once Gordy moves out of earshot, Emory leans over and says, "That was one brilliant move, even if I do say so myself. Giving that fifty grand back killed any thoughts the FBI had about us cheating all those old folks."

Emory tries to pat himself on the back, but fails and only gets the shoulder, and spills half his drink doing it. Randle just laughs, bumps the stool, and then spills his entire drink down his pants. He quickly grabs some napkins and blots at the stains, stumbling around nearly out of control. Both men burst out laughing.

Gordy says, "Time to head home boys. We're done for the day." Gordy grabs the car keys off the bar. "And no driving, you both walk home or I'll call you a ride with a badge on it." The bartender shakes his head, understanding he made a major error in the pour today. "Make that a stagger home." Gordy waves them both out the door.

Emory and Randle wobble a wide circle around the building and sneak up on the BMW. Emory fishes up under the right rear fender, extracts a spare key, and unlocks the door. The sporty vehicle weaves a little as it heads north along the highway toward the condo he rents month to month just a mile away. Emory decided he needs distance between his home and his offices in the next county, and EATS 'n DRINKS has become his favorite watering hole and pick-up bar lately.

"There they go," Ellie says. Dressed in new clothing befitting her investor role, she sits behind the wheel in a rented Jaguar XKR that sets the group back three thousand dollars for six weeks. That makes four thousand altogether including the clothing and hair styling, and miscellaneous items that remove the vagabond look, and adds several burner phones.

Ellie and Tick watch the BMW weave down the highway. Ellie eases out onto the pavement behind the two fraudsters and follows a safe distance behind.

"Both pretty drunk, looks like," Tick says. "Bartender probably grabbed the keys. Emory dug out the spare."

* * *

The next day, Tick and Ellie slide into a booth at EATS 'n DRINKS and check out the lunch menu. The mid-day crowd fills half the room and a few regulars line the bar, keeping the bartender busy pouring drinks and shaking for music.

The cup hits the bar upside down, the dice rule, and the loser slides a dollar into the slot, selects two tunes. The mood seems soft and bluesy today, a little surprising with the country look of the customers. Apparently, farmers and ranchers enjoy the blues as much as they do Merle and Travis. One of the best guitarists in the history of music captures the room, an Eric Clapton acoustic tune encourages finger taps and bouncing knees.

Two coffee cups and several stacks of official looking papers cover the table top. Ellie says, "Okay, we know they come here often, and we know where they live."

"We hardly ever see them here together though. Wonder why?"

"Don't know. Maybe they just don't want to be seen together. Emory comes often, but we've seen Randle only twice in two weeks and never with Emory. They're probably playing it careful after all that's happened," Ellie says.

'Yeah, after my brother, then his buddy flipping into the river. I'm surprised either one stuck around. I'd be long gone in his shoes if he's as crooked as we think."

The waitress checks back."First time here?" A thin middle-aged waitress wearing jeans and a house sweatshirt with EATS 'n DRINKS printed across the front pulls her lips into a pout, grabs a pencil out of her hair, and says, "Try our ham and cheese, it's the best around, and we cook the fries in spiced oil that makes you drool, even after you finish."

Ellie falls for the pitch, and orders, "Yes, first time, we're here on business. Two plates and a refill here." She points at the empty cups. "One more cup, we got a friend coming. We'll eat after she leaves." The waitress turns up a third cup, fills all three and disappears.

Tick lifts a page off one stack, compares it to another, makes a few comments, low and secretive, and looks around as if daring anyone to eavesdrop. No one cares. He continues the act, taking no chances and playing his part right alongside Ellie.

A blue and white pickup kicks gravel up in the lot and bumps a wooden curb outside a large picture window that fronts the restaurant. A woman dressed in black pants and shirt, covered by a dark winter coat exits the truck, Frankie remains in his seat, the truck idling and heater running. Twin plumes of smoke float out duel exhaust pipes. A nearly identical plume of moist breath blows into the mist as Annie quick-steps toward the entry and carries the scent of frost inside with her.

All eyes turn toward the door swinging in, and then turn away when a strange woman none of the locals recognize enters. Annie looks around, spots Tick and Ellie, joins them at the table. Annie wraps her fingers around the extra cup and warms her hands, takes a sip, and starts talking quietly. Tick flips over the top page on each stack, so Annie can read it. Three voices confer briefly, the words soft, low, and secretive, as if hiding a conspiracy from the customers.

Working back and forth behind the bar, Gordy alternates his pour with the dice game, and occasionally flicks his eyes over toward the table and watches his new visitors. Curious, but never prying, Gordy checks out all his customers, new and old, strangers or locals. That's what a good bartender and business owners do, keep an eye on the clientele, stay on top of the needs. Gordy's good at both tending bar and running his business.

He knows who benefits his operation, and who doesn't. Gordy embraces new business, and tolerates no rowdiness in his establishment. Locals know it, and new customers realize it quickly. Gordy flops the cup and glances over at the table, recognizing a business deal in progress. He glances at the dice, slides a dollar in the slot, punches up a Patsy Cline tune, hits another selection and turns back to the bar.

Far from the majority of homeless derelicts that haunt the streets of our cities, or rail yard camps, this team looks and acts exactly like what it is now -- intelligent victims of circumstance smart enough to work together and seek retribution. It easily becomes dressy and fancy for a month, or longer, and certainly long enough to pull off this trick. Scam the scammer, the group slogan lights up the dawn every morning while the clan sits around the burn barrel and plans its day.

Ellie offers her hand. Annie shakes it. Ellie removes the top two pages out of each stack and Annie scribbles her name on all six pages, then Ellie repeats it on each. Ellie removes a wallet from her fanny pack, writes out a check, signs it and hands it to Annie. A smile splits her face when Annie accepts the check, and her signed documents.

Annie shakes hands with Tick, says a few more words and retreats out the same door she entered fifteen minutes ago, grinning all the way as if she just won the lottery. She climbs into the pickup.

Tick and Ellie watch the classic GMC back away, and bump fists. The remaining pages disappear into Ellie's backpack. Thirty seconds later, the plates arrive and two coffee cups gain another refill.

Ellie pops a French fry into her mouth, "Mmmmm, wow, that's different." The excellent spiced flavor proves the waitress told the truth. "Better have another." Gordy's magic kitchen strikes again. Another fry disappears between her lips.

* * *

Two days later, as evening approaches, Annie wraps Ellie up in a hug, "You take care of yourself. This guy ain't to be trusted. Keep that phone on and punch the Junkie button if you need us." Annie points at the GMC sitting up on the gravel patch above the culvert, right next to the Jaguar. "Frankie's says he'll be ready and waiting if you call."

Frankie says, "Captain told me to follow you in ten minutes, so me and Tick will be close. Number one is ICE, number two will get Junkie and Annie, number three will get Frankie and Tick in the truck two minutes away. We'll be down the road from EATS just in case."

"Don't you dare leave with him without calling," Annie says, "so Frankie and Tick can follow."

"Don't worry about me. I can take care of myself." Ellie aims a grin at Annie. "Been fending off vultures like this one for half my twenty-eight years on earth, and the farm boys too." Dressed in a set of professional level clothing she bought at a thrift store just for this event and the false business meeting with Tick and Annie at the bar, Ellie grabs her new designer bag. "Well, most of them farm boys anyway grins at Annie."

Tick and Frankie watch Ellie climb the hill. Frankie says, "Cleans up right nice, don't she, Tick."

Annie bats Frankie lightly across the back of his head. "You shut that mouth."

Frankie glances at his tree, rubs the stub face in his pocket. "Captain said it, not me. I was just agreeing." That comment gets a chuckle from all three.

The Jaguar spins a U-turn and aims north toward EATS 'n DRINKS. Thirty minutes later, she parks and pushes in through the door, picks out a stool at the end of a nearly full bar, the regular Friday night crowd. "Scotch and water," she says when Gordy drops a napkin in front of her.

"Coming right up." A glass and ice appears almost immediately, and a heavy pour. Gordy begins a conversation with Ellie while serving his barmaid and three couples and four single men at the bar, and checking out what might become a new regular customer.

Intermittently, Gordy and Ellie swap everyday get to know you chatter. Ellie sips her drink minimally, keeping her mind clear. Gordy asks, "You new in town?"

"Yup. Here on business, meeting a client."

"What kind of business, if you don't mind my asking?"

"Real estate development. We're doing preliminary for a project."

"Where at?"

Ellie looks at him, rolls her eyes. "You're kidding, right?"

The bartender laughs, "Yeah, just trying to get a little advance notice, sneak in a piece of the action.

Forget I asked." Both share an intimate chuckle at that one.

Gordy points at her glass and Ellie nods a yes just as the door swings open and Emory steps in. He climbs on the one remaining open stool at the other end of the bar. Gordy sets a glass and pours. Ellie ignores Emory but discretely follows the scene in the bar mirror.

Emory says, "Hey Gordy, you seen John lately."

"Not since Tuesday. He never comes in much anyway, and even less since his buddy drowned in the river."

Fifteen minutes passes uneventfully. Two different men ask Ellie to dance when the music hits a slow, country waltz twice in a row after several rowdy cowboy tunes. She refuses both, and they eventually leave her alone. Gordy parks in front of her for a moment, asks Ellie if Emory can buy her a drink. She covers her half empty glass and shakes her head no.

Unwilling to accept defeat so easily on a Friday night and alone, Emory decides he better pursue this one on his own. Gordy points a thumb up toward Emory, but Emory shakes off the bet. He's missed two in a row and needs a winner before he bets again. He struts along behind the stools, introduces himself. "Cal Emory. Can I get you another scotch?"

Her eyes track up and down, as if evaluating him and the offer, "Nope, never accept a drink from strangers."

Emory pushes a little, pulling up his usual self-serving lines, but Ellie turns back to the bar. "Besides,

I'm leaving." She empties her glass, tosses a couple bills on the bar, slides off the stool and heads for the door.

"At least let me walk you out." Emory follows her for three or four steps.

Ellie sticks a little grit in her voice this time. "I don't know you, Clint. But if you take one step out that door when I go through it, my first call will be to my brother, the second will be to the ambulance to come pick you up off the dirt outside after he gets here."

"Cal," he says. "It's Cal," He pops his palms up in a hold it pose, "Okay, okay." His eyes track Ellie out the door, across the front window and watch her unlock the sporty bronze Jaguar coupe she rented specifically for hustling Emory. She looks and acts the role she plays, a savvy business woman.

Emory returns to his stool. Gordy laughs, sets a tumbler on the bar and pours scotch over the ice, "Good thing you didn't bet."

"Very nice," Emory says, "and she drives a brand new Jag."

"Once again, Carlton, you're thinking with your dick instead of your brain, and it ain't the first time," Gordy says. "Look where it got you last time. Paying off that dancer and abortion fees, even more because she waited. Pretty expensive lay, you ask me."

Emory slides a frown on his face. "Feisty bitch, though. Seen her in here before?"

"Just once. Come in couple days ago with a tall guy, early thirties, not local. Another woman came in later. Looked like they were doing some kind of business deal. Signed a few papers, one wrote a check.

The woman took it and left, skipping out the door like she scored big time. Never seen any of them before that."

Outside, Ellie slips in behind the wheel and blows out a breath, but she can't quite hold back a smile. "Gottcha." She heads back to the hobo camp and hides the Jaguar inside the Monahan barn, along with the GM truck. Sue and Arnold think she inherited it from her aunt and she's protecting it from the weather until she sells it. The less people that know about the retaliation plan, the better. A group decision.

* * *

"Yeah, a perfect gentleman underneath all that sleaze," Annie says, and pokes a stick at the fire. "Here, you need this one." She offers a brown glass pint. "Did you really call him Clint?" Her signature giggle once again echoes into the trees. "Excellent!"

Ellie takes a long pull then coughs. "Yup, sure did, will set that final hook tomorrow or next day."

"Well, we wrote the first chapter in the book," Tick adds. "Now we just gotta push it on through to the end."

"We'll get there, right Captain?" Frankie yells over his shoulder, looks at his face tree as if expecting an answer. Shrugs it off when he hears nothing, mutters, "Must be sleeping."

Tick offers a short overview of the information he and Ellie gathered. "It's been two weeks since we launched this plan. We know he hangs out at EATS. We know he calls himself Cal and considers himself a lady's man, as we've seen him leave EATS numerous times with different women, some new, some repeats. And, he hit on Ellie the first time she showed up alone. We know where he lives, an upscale condo at the Riverside Resort. We also know he's full of himself, thinks the world owes him anything he wants."

Ellie continues, "We know his partner lives at the Fort Freeman building, also pretty high bucks. So we know they have money and spend it pretty freely, probably mostly from the scams they pull off. We know one partner, Cliff Patterson or what's his name, flipped into the river and had fake identification. So, we can't be sure about real names for either one."

Frankie says, "Don't matter what they call themselves as long as we can find them when we want. And Ellie or Tick followed both home several times, so it's not temporary. Both rent though, there's no title in any name we know. In both cases, land titles at town hall show each building still belongs to the original developer."

"Come pick me up Frankie." Frankie hops in his pickup and follows Ellie in the Jaguar. She's parking the Jaguar temporarily inside Sue and Arnold Monahan's barn, eliminating the chance Emory might drive past some day and recognize it. The plan might have a few holes in it, but Emory accidentally finding the Jaguar won't be one.

Frankie bought a tarp, and hides his truck in the trees for the same reason.

Chapter Twenty-three

After receiving a phone call from Deputy Joe, the coroner arrives at the Fort Freeman apartment building. He parks next to a white Blazer with a gold badge decorating its door. Standing in the parking lot a minute or two, he looks up at a second floor patio deck. Water drips intermittently off the edge and dribbles down into a brick planter below.

He heads for the entrance, climbs the stairs, enters the apartment, and says, "What've you got, Joe."

"Prelim only. Wet floor, soap suds, open booze bottle, fresh cut and swelling on his forehead. Looks like he slipped and the tub wall knocked him out. He slid under the water, unconscious. Faucet kept filling until it ran over. Manager called me when he opened the door to see why water was flooding out the deck, and he found this guy bent over face-down in the tub wearing a towel."

"Know who he is?"

"Manager says John Randle, rented it two months ago. License in his pants matches the name, but he's not local. Somewhere in Idaho."

Sitting in his office the next morning, the coroner hands Deputy Joe the field report and autopsy. The coroner begins interpreting it while Joe follows on his copies.

"Drowned in the tub, looks like he started filling it, slipped on the wet floor. Tub wall knocked him out, maybe. Nasty injury in the temple area. Didn't kill him but appears he whacked his head, fell on his knees, hit the edge or maybe the faucet and landed face first in the tub, unconscious."

The coroner points at x-rays set on a light window. Three very close-in exposures show the injury, a skull fracture above the right ear. "Half empty bottle of vodka on the scene, and alcohol in his blood. High enough content to make him pretty unstable."

"Or, could've done it if he slipped backwards, and his head hit the edge of the tub on the way down, too, and he tipped over. We found him lying on his face in the tub, underwater. So that all works in this scene. And, water in his lungs, certainly enough for a drowning. He might've slipped, knocked himself out and sucked in the water. Never woke up."

"Filler spout was splashing right beside his head, too. Weird how he fell, his head partially blocked the drain fitting. Water rose up but drained out nearly as fast as the spout filling it. Looks like it took a couple hours before the manager noticed water running out on the patio deck and off onto the walkway."

"In fact, in my official medical opinion, that's exactly what happened. Drunk, fell, knocked himself out, and drowned. Not sure my gut agrees with it though."

Deputy Joe says, "Did these two men know one another, I wonder? Seems weird to have two strangers in town die an unnatural death without some connection. Both from Idaho, but different towns. Though both seem like accidents, this makes me doubt the other one a bit more now."

The coroner flips through the pages again, holds up a photo. "Got no idea, will check around and see. You should ask Gordy, too. He knows most everybody. And if he don't know him personally, most anybody comes around eats at EATS at least a few times, even visitors."

"This one's a tough call, Joe. One guy flips into the river, another guy falls in the tub. Could go either way, but got no reason to think someone murdered either one. We don't even know this one and nothing local on his prints. FBI won't get back to us any time soon. That IAFIS search takes forever if you ain't federal."

"We get one homicide a year, average. Now four homicides this year. Shelly Packard finally shotgunned her boyfriend last month, for beating her and her kids. No surprise there," Deputy Joe says. "Asshole had it coming, damn near took his head off. She'll walk on that one with a little counseling. Showed up in court with bruises on her back and ribs, and a black eye, one tooth knocked out. Don't blame her at all."

"Then the hobo gets beat up, the fake Patterson guy flips off the bridge. Now this one, dead taking a bath. First time in ten years we got more than one homicide in a year, let alone two accidents a month apart, and both a bit odd. Plus the thug triplets beating a guy down at the hobo camp."

"A bit freaky, I'd say" The coroner pulls the rubber sheet up over John Randle and slides the drawer back into cold storage. "Makes me wonder about all of it."

"Think I'll take a much closer peek at both these accidents, a real close look. Maybe pull in some help from the district to give us some more eyes and ears. Could be Sheriff Johnson can push the FBI a bit, see if they'll at least rush the prints, and try a larger data base search. We mostly get local and greater Chicago."

Both men hear a door open, turn and look at the entrance to the morgue. Scott Monroe steps in and says, "What you got here, Jack?"

"A puzzle," Deputy Joe answers for the coroner then laughs. "Maybe it's a mob hit. We got anything the mob needs here. Couple bulls maybe, cow or two." All three men join in a brief chuckle.

"Tell me," Scott says. They tell him. Coroner hands one copy to Scott Monroe and says, "Read this. Can't officially let you keep it Scott, against the rules."

Then he grins. "Won't know it if you find a couple extra pages on that desk outside the office when you leave though. Seems Marilyn ran a copy or two more than we actually need."

Scott says nothing, but tips his fingers to his forehead, a silent thank you salute. Small town folks working together to right some wrongs, bend a few rules when they can get away with it.

Chapter Twenty-four

Dressed like rich folks they've never been, Tick and Frankie stand at a tall work table inside an office and chat with an architect. Another trip to the local church thrift store based near Wheaton College west of Chicago gave both men an upscale and professional appearance, nearly unrecognizable from the hobo camp gruffness a few days ago. Definitely worth a tiny hit to the operating budget.

Benny Reed lays out a preliminary set of drawings showing a road layout, and parking, and a series of lots and building sites across an imaginary fifty acre parcel of slightly rolling, partly flat, and dipping patch of land outside the Chicago city and Cook County lines about a hundred and twenty miles, an imaginary distance as well. "How's that layout look?" Benny asks. "That about what you want?"

"Perfect," Frankie responds, appraising the plot plan. His engineering degree from MIT earned him a commission in the Army sixteen years ago. He served almost fourteen years as a field officer in Special Forces before the grenade explosion in Panama cost him a foot, and supplied him with a fuzzy brain and a medical discharge.

Another set of drawings illustrates a major highway plan that runs off an imaginary new cloverleaf exiting I-80 and running south, straight at the acreage. Neither plan shows any identifiable location markers. "The highway design too. Excellent."

"Wish you could tell me more about this development plan," Benny Reed says. "I could give you a better idea about costs and the potential for this getting cleared by the state and the feds. You guys have a great idea here, expensive, but a great idea."

"We're still in discussions with the sellers, and want to keep this location private until we close the deal, and own it. The seller accepted a contingent offer based on us satisfying engineering, environmental reports, and the feasibility of getting some big box and large mall vendors signed first. The next closest medical center sits fifty six miles north, and the closest one south, sixty-two. The town's begging for this one but we need preliminary drawings so we can float the concept in front of the right people."

Tick says. "Some can envision it. Some need papers with lines and dots."

Frankie adds, "For now, that's under wraps until we're sure." He reaches into his pocket, rubs his oak idol, receives approval for the lie. "Once we get further along with finance and the regulators, we'll get you the locations."

"Okay," says Reed, "You're tying my hands, but you're the boss. I can have these drawing and spec's copied for delivery by tomorrow. Jennie told me artist renderings and elevations for the buildings will be ready then, too."

"Fine," Tick says. "We'll bring a check."

Everyone shakes hands around, and small time Benny Reed smiles at the dollar signs he imagines in his future. Lead architect on a major mall and medical center development. The thought of it makes his heart sing and his feet twitch, but he stands completely still, hiding his emotion, giving nothing away.

Tick slips into the passenger seat. Frankie backs his truck out, heads toward the hobo encampment, a seventy mile drive, grins over at Tick. "Hope he don't get too disappointed when he never sees us again."

"He'll get a nice fat eighteen hundred bucks tomorrow for drawing a series of imaginary lines on a few sheets of graph paper and printing a few photo-shopped building images. That's enough. We got all we need," Tick says.

Frankie grins and adds, "That's a nice touch across the bottom of all those drawings and art renderings. Broderick and Heath Engineering and Development, LLC in big old blue script. Adds a little class to our project."

Chapter Twenty-five

Concerned about three days and no calls or visits at the office, Emory aims the BMW toward the Fort Freeman apartments. Ten minutes later, he stands on the sidewalk and listens to the manager explain about John Randle and the tub accident.

"Cops asked me about friends, but I had no idea how to reach you. I saw you with John a few times, but he has no contacts listed on his lease. I recognize you and your car, but had no way to call."

The news hits him hard as John has been a great partner and lucrative salesman for the last few years, and as much a friend as one can become when two untrustworthy men engage in dishonest projects together.

Briefly, the oddity crosses his mind about two accidental deaths within such a short time. Eventually, his ego and selfishness shrug that thought away as irrelevant.

Emory believes he's above reproach or harm from anyone, and that accidents happen only to others. He accepts it as a strange coincidence, because that suits him and he can ignore it. He basks in the good fortune that his partners lost their lives in untimely incidents for both but very timely incidents for him. He figures it's just the luck he deserves, and that destiny tripled his net worth in less than a month without him lifting a finger.

A week ago, Randle and Emory consolidated some funds into one investment account, just over a million dollars, left almost two million offshore, temporarily.

Today, Emory owns it all, the accounts, the new business, and the fruits that remain from all the investment fraud, including a small office suite in the next county he'd bought for his personal use. Emory has never operated any scams out of it and neither of his partners knew he'd bought it, or the luxury townhouse he owns right on the lakeshore between Chicago and Milwaukee.

A completely clean office building, Emory believes, and it's true. Only Emory knows of its existence at the moment, excepting Harold. His long-time security man maintains both, and hires lawn and cleaning people weekly.

Once a month Harold heads into Chicago and upkeeps the townhouse. His special treat to himself, he spends the night in a hotel down on State Street and buys a woman for the evening. Even as a young man, Harold never had much luck with the ladies, never married, and remains a life-long sexist and an unsophisticated predator.

Emory holds the titles in his name only, pays the taxes and maintenance bills out of a private account. He bought the properties years ago, paid cash, keeps both separate from all his crooked activities. He's saved these two for his retirement, although now he figures it's safe to run Green Pastures alone out of the office building. It's completely clean, as is the new company he plans to run legally out of these suites.

With these sudden riches, he figures he can retire in the lavish style he deserves anywhere he chooses in another year or two, and never work again. Emory decides he'll operate the new real estate company by himself, believes no one can find him, and that his new and legitimate business will never track back to all the scams he ran.

The posh leather seat settles comfortably beneath him. A slimy slug at peace with the world, Emory smiles and points the BMW at his favorite haunt. "Pour a scotch for me, Gordy, and toast a new and completely independent self," he whispers to no one in particular. "Time for a walk first."

He exits Fort Freeman parking lot and turns left toward the state recreation area two miles from his condo. He wanders same nature trail each morning before he hits the office. He's a little late today, but suddenly has a lot on his mind. Upbeat due to his newfound wealth, he ignores the loss of his partners and begins planning a new life.

Ellie and Tick sit in a tan Toyota Celica Tick rented for one week just to follow Emory without him recognizing the Jaguar. Tick pulls out behind him, and turns the opposite direction. "There he goes. He's driving the black one today and heading toward the park. You're up Ellie."

Tick pulls into a mini-mall parking lot and Ellie jumps out, slides in behind the wheel of the Jaguar she'd parked there earlier, exits the lot, and aims it toward the recreation area.

Ten minutes later Ellie jogs along a pathway that circles a small pond with a few oaks and pines sprinkled along its shore. She spots Emory quickly, hands in his pockets, casually roaming along a short developed trail eight feet wide that meanders through the forest and skirts the pond, a course she now knows he follows nearly every day when he visits this park.

Emory turns his back to the pond and stretches. A trim, fit runner in green jogging sweats heads his way, short red curls bouncing each time a shoe hits the ground. As Ellie closes in, he recognizes her from that bar. His eyes rise in greeting, a slick smile spreads across his face, and he waves a hand.

Ellie ignores him, her steady jogger pace rhythmic and true.

Emory steps into the middle of the path and holds up a palm in greeting, as if to stop her. "Hey," he shouts.

She runs right on past, skirting along one side on the trail. Her bright blue eyes capture his very briefly as she passes but she keeps running. About fifteen feet beyond Emory, Ellie wiggles her fingers over her right shoulder without looking back and continues the same pace down the dirt path.

Five minutes later she hits the parking lot and hops into the Jaguar as Emory puffs into the lot behind her, not quite keeping up. The sporty bronze coupe kicks up a bit of gravel and spins out the entrance. Ellie aims it south toward the hobo camp thirty minutes away.

"Perfect." She grins, and pumps her fist. She peeks in the mirror and spots Emory standing in the dirt, hands on his hips, staring. The Jaguar accelerates down the highway and disappears around a curve.

Chapter Twenty-six

Early the next morning, a husky, dark-haired woman wearing a stylish gray suit with a gold badge hanging off its pocket and a Glock on her hip pushes into the entrance at the office building Emory recently opened. A new sign above the door reads Green Pastures Real Estate and Development.

Deputy Joe follows her in. Harold takes one look at the uniform and the badge, picks up the phone and punches a speed dial.

A green Blazer wheels into the parking lot a minute or two later than the driver planned. Scott Monroe hops out, grabs a notebook and a camera. He quickly trots in behind Deputy Joe and observes but says nothing.

The woman points a wallet and identification card at Harold Bunny and says, "FBI. Brenda Davis, Financial Investigations. Put it down ... Now!"

Harold obliges, disconnects the phone, almost raises his hands but catches himself in the nick of time. No sense in admitting awareness of guilt before she tells him what she wants. He settles back in his seat. "What's this all about?" As if he doesn't know.

"Keep your hands where I can see them." Harold lays his arms on the counter, fingers out flat. An ex-cop, he remembers the drill. "Where's Carlton Emory? We need to speak with him."

"Ain't here."

"You know where he is, or when he'll be here?"

"Nope. I just mind the phone."

"Yeah, right! We'll see about that, Mister Bunny."

Harold arches his eyebrows, surprised she called him by his name. A little worry skitters across his face, but he knows enough about cops and investigators to keep his mouth shut.

"We have subpoenas for all financial records dating back six years, and an order for Mister Emory to appear at a federal hearing." She drops a large yellow envelope on his desktop. "Consider Carlton Emory served."

"He's not here, and I can't accept service."

Special Agent Brenda Davis doesn't even bat an eye and calls his bluff. "You're his agent, if you can sign for UPS, you can accept service."

She lays an identical envelope beside the first. "Consider yourself served too. Harold Bunny, you're ordered to show up at the same time, next Friday morning, ten o'clock. Don't miss it or we'll come back and find you, and arrest you both."

Scott Monroe aims his camera, shoots several photos of the agent confronting the security man and handing him the envelopes.

"Unlock his office," Deputy Joe finally breaks his silence.

"I can't do that. Mister Emory's not here."

The agent shakes her head, as if talking to a child. "Nope, not good enough. Unlock it now. If we open it ourselves, he won't like the extra expense." She aims a finger out the entrance. A second agent stands beside the FBI vehicle holding a heavy steel cylinder equipped to open locked doors. A very effective tool.

Harold stares at both officers a moment, glances once more at the parking lot and the dark gray battering ram. He thinks it through for about two seconds and grabs his keys. He leads the way and unlocks the office then watches Davis and Deputy Joe search two filing cabinets with nothing inside but building ownership documents and a few real estate listings and some development zoning laws.

Davis sits in a fancy leather chair and pops open the drawers on a Brazilian Rosewood desk, a fine piece of furniture. It reveals a few personal items, again nothing of interest and no evidence of financial fraud.

"Fuck!" Davis slams her fist down in the desktop, venting her frustration at missing the target. "He knew we were coming." She guesses incorrectly. Emory never keeps incriminating documents in a building where he operates his scams, especially this new and clean building. He hides all paperwork in a storage unit rented under a completely different fake name and paid from a different bank account.

Deputy Joe and the FBI agent retreat out the door. Davis bumps a fist with Scott Monroe. "Thanks for the heads-up Scott, gives us just enough to go after these animals. Nothing here now, but we'll get more next week in the courtroom."

Already dialing, Harold Bunny watches both vehicles spin out onto the highway.

Simultaneous to the events occurring at the Green Pastures office building, Thomas Hargrove and a junior FBI agent he's training knock on a door at the Riverside Resort condo complex. The door swings open. Hargrove holds out his badge and bullies his way inside, his arrogance and belligerent attitude clearly exhibiting itself. He trips over a throw rug and nearly falls on his face, barely catching himself on table inside the entry.

Red-faced at his own clumsiness and feeling foolish with his trainee present, Hargrove barks, "Subpoena," and hands over copies of the same papers Brenda Davis served Harold Bunny at the real estate office. "And search warrant!"

Emory jambs his phone on his ear, "Emory here!" He listens for two or three seconds. "Yeah, Harold, they just arrived."

He disconnects and, without thinking, accepts the documents then suddenly collects himself, installs a little rage in his attitude, throws the paperwork against the wall and yells, "Get out! You have no right to come in here uninvited! Get the hell out of my house."

"Yes, we do have a right. Read it. Sit your ass down over there while we search. You move off that couch, I'll stick these pretty steel bracelets on your wrists and chain you to that doorknob." Handcuffs hang on his belt right beside a Glock handgun.

Thirty minutes later Hargrove glares at his partner, shakes his head and says, "Nothing," and then grins at Emory. "See you next Friday."

The door swings shut. Emory elevates his middle finger, aims it at the door as the agents exit. He immediately pulls out his cell phone, punches in a number.

"Get Lester." He listens briefly. "Break into it. I need him on the phone now!" A few seconds pass. "What? Okay, ten minutes. No longer!"

His phone dings almost as soon as he disconnects. "Lester," he barks into the mouthpiece. "Oh, no. Thought you were someone else." He listens a moment. "What do you mean, 'Frozen and overdrawn' ... Who? ... Well unfreeze it and pay the checks."

Emory listens for almost a minute. "You can't? That's why you're my personal banker, so you can!" He slams the phone shut.

The phone dings again. "What now?" He listens. "About time, Lester. The damn FBI served me a subpoena and a warrant, just now, searched my home and office, and froze my bank account. My rent check and the BMW insurance payment bounced."

He raises his voice, almost screaming into the phone. "Damn it, get my money released and get this court thing squashed before Friday! Call Martin, get him to kick the subpoena and the appearance."

Emory listens again briefly, his anger taking control. "You can't? He can't? It takes time? Well, why the fuck do I pay you guys so much?"

He slams the receiver shut and fires it across the room. The phone bounces off the oak banister and shatters. He jumps up and kicks a chair then screams in pain, hobbles around in a circle on one foot then falls back on the couch, rubbing his ankle.

* * *

Forty minutes later Deputy Joe slides down the gravel embankment and approaches the hobo camp. Annie brushes two inches of overnight snowfall off the woodpile and works on building up the fire. She waves a glove at him.

"Ellie and Tick around?"

"Yep, over there collecting kindling."

She points and hollers. Ellie and Tick each grab an armload of forest debris, carry it over and dump it next to the burn barrel.

Deputy Joe says, "FBI just served papers on the guy that ripped off your family. He's set to appear in court next Friday at ten. You might want to show up. Looks like Scott Monroe skipped over that clown Hargrove and finally got the boss involved."

Joe explains Agent Brenda Davis, the offices, the condo, what happened this morning, the subpoena service, the warrants, and a minor amount of background.

"Another senior couple complained to FBI about that Porter slash Patterson guy, the one that drove into the river a couple weeks ago. Apparently, the wife has some family political juice and got action up the ladder."

"Then Scott Monroe somehow connected him to a guy named Carlton Emory. Got another one too. Scott tied a shyster named John Reardon, aka John Randle, together with both Emory and the Patterson guy. One flipped off the bridge and broke his neck, one drowned in his tub."

"So now we got three scammers working together and ripping off seniors, two accidentally dead under odd circumstances, and only a month apart. Emory's the last."

Ellie says, "Looks like this guy Clint Emory might be eliminating his partners and keeping the all the pie." Tick rolls his eyes at her use of the name Clint, but then understands she's kicking at any possibility Deputy Joe might think she knows Emory.

"Carlton, not Clint," Joe says. "Calls himself Cal according to Scott Monroe. Scott's at his office if you want to go talk with him."

"Davis might send you a subpoena too but more likely they'll ask Gina and Mickey. If not, I'd gather all the papers you have and give Brenda Davis a call directly."

Joe hands Tick a slip of paper. "Here's her private line. Stay away from Hargrove. Just go direct to Brenda now. She's hot-lining this case." The deputy trudges back up the hill and hops into his vehicle.

Tick says, "Damn, damn, damn! Busted by the feds!" He kicks at the ground so hard he slips and falls backwards into a snowdrift. Annie bursts out laughing.

Ellie can't help it, and loses it right along with Annie. Both struggle to contain it and finally stop. Then Tick flairs his arms into a snow angel and bursts out laughing too. "Did that look as dumb as it felt?"

The giggling starts it all over again, Annie and her telltale screech accenting the humor. Tick climbs to his feet and dusts the white crystals off his pants.

"That sure puts a tweak in our plan," he says. "We'll never get at his money now."

Ellie wanders around in a circle, concentrating, working on this new dilemma.

"This kind of court processing usually takes time, not overnight. We'll see what happens Friday, meantime, we escalate our schedule. We still have five days. We'll keep that tail on him and catch him at EATS, see what he has to say when I accidentally run into him again."

Tick whips out his burner phone and dials. "I'll extend the Honda rental a week."

"I know what Joe said, but no way can I show up in court. Can't let Emory tie me to the scams he ran, just in case. And that'll sure do it. I'll let my grandparents know, and their attorney. They'll get the falsified documents to the FBI as easily as I can, and that won't expose me to that slimy fraudster."

"Besides, it was their farm and money, not mine. No reason for the FBI to serve papers on me, or even know about me. I'll tell Granny and Gramps to forget that part, don't bring my name up at all."

* * *

Tick and Ellie sit in the rented Honda across from the Riverside Resort that same afternoon, watching the silver BMW sports car this time. Tick says, "Same routine pretty much every day since he lost his partners."

Emory leaves home at nine, heads for the park, takes a walk then heads for his new office. Hangs out there a while, hits EATS for lunch, back to the office then hits EATS middle of the afternoon, and hangs out until he heads home for the night. Once in a while he takes a woman home with him, but no one permanent, sometimes the same one, occasionally a new one. He's caught in a spiral since he lost his partners. He's hung up on routine, and he never meets a client. Not in his office, not at a home. It's like he can't make a decision so he marches in place, accomplishing nothing.

"I should hit him tonight. We only have four days before court."

"Okay, let's get the Jag, and tell Annie. Be better if we're sitting at EATS when he gets there today. We can play it out."

* * *

Tick and Annie sit across from Ellie in a booth. A few papers lie on the table. Emory pulls into the

EATS 'n DRINKS, parks between a blue and white classic pickup and a bronze Jaguar. He takes a second look at the Jaguar and smiles. He enters, sits at the bar in his regular stool. Gordy slaps a napkin down and pours. Emory takes a sip and angles his eyes around the room, spots Ellie, turns away quickly, unsure how to handle it as she rejected him twice and stepped right in the middle of his ego.

After about ten minutes of low volume heated discussion, Ellie shoves some papers across the table and barks, "So what? We're already on agreement."

Annie grabs the papers, jumps up and stomps out the door. Tick tosses a few bills on the table and follows her out, a bit of anger in his stride. They hop into the blue and white pickup and depart, Tick driving.

Ellie sips her coffee, and after a minute, looks up and finds Emory standing at her table. "Hi," he says, "it's me, from here last week, and at the park the other day."

"Yeah, I remember. I was out jogging."

"Pretty cold out there."

"I was running, you were walking. Big difference."

Emory laughs. "You're right. I should run or stay home. Can I buy you a drink, now that we're not strangers?"

Ellie ponders the offer, as if she might refuse him again. "Coffee refill will do it."

Emory waves at Gordy, points at her cup, raises his glass, and squeezes into the booth across from Ellie.

In less than a minute Gordy brings a coffee pot and another scotch. Half hour later, after the traditional 'Where are you from? What do you do?' introductions, the coffee turns into a scotch and water for both, then another.

Later still and into the third round, Emory says, "So what was that argument about, those two seemed a little upset?"

"Nothing. A little business deal falling off track, a financing issue. Not open for discussion." Ellie tips up her drink, slides out of the booth. "Gotta go."

Emory follows her out. Ellie unlocks the Jaguar, climbs in and rolls down the window. "Thanks for the drinks, nice to meet you." A smile brightens her face and her eyes sparkle like she means it. She doesn't.

"How about dinner tomorrow?"

Ellie opens a small daybook, shakes her head. "Make it lunch. Here, noon."

She squeals out onto the highway and disappears around a curve. Smitten like never before in his life, Emory turns back toward the bar, swings a fist. "Yes!"

He puffs out his chest, whips out his phone and dials. "Lester, my office, a half hour." The answer drags a frown across his face. "All right, two hours."

* * *

Back at his office, Emory sits behind his desk across from Lester Steinmann. The attorney says,

"Martin can't do anything this fast. He needs time. These are feds, Cal."

"So what? He's a fed too, a judge. That makes him one of them, and one of us. He pockets my cash fast enough, both of you, and a lot of it."

Emory blows out a breath. "All right Lester. For right now, by tomorrow, you set up a trust without my name anywhere on it. But I want access to the funds whenever I need it. Use the Richard Bailey identity. It's clean, never been used. Soon as you do it, I'll transfer the rest of the Green Pastures offshore accounts here. I need money. The feds froze me out."

"Attorney fees, expenses, my condo rent, the Beamers. Gotta eat. Gotta drink. Gotta play. Feds make the rules. Tie up my funds so I can't fight back. No wonder they win in court, they strangle the opponents."

"I'll try."

"No try. Do it Lester, or I'll find someone who can. You guys piss around so much and cost me a fortune. Might as well go legit, pay taxes. Less headaches."

* * *

At ten minutes before noon, Emory wheels into the lot and parks his black BMW beside the bronze Jaguar, grins into the mirror and pats his hair into place. A minute later, he slides in a booth across from Ellie. Small talk takes up the order and lunch time.

Ellie pushes her plate away. "Great fries here."

"Yup, famous for that. Gordy's secret recipe." Emory slides his coffee cup aside, signals Gordy with two fingers, and a thumb up. As if the bartender could read minds and create magic, the plates and cups disappear and two brandies arrive, over ice.

"So, you gonna tell me about your finance problem? Maybe I can help, I know a few folks around here with some influence, and a little money."

Ellie glances around, catches his eye then glances around again, as if indecisive.

"Okay. That woman here yesterday? She's a federal legislature assistant. She operates land sales and acquisitions for the feds, mostly wilderness and wetlands. We brokered a deal to auction off a parcel of land currently under federal protection. The guy was with her holds my development contract, under a contingency."

"Anytime federal land goes up for sale, it must go to auction and open bids. And, the buyer must supply like-quantity wilderness or wetlands elsewhere so the feds keep the same amount of land under the national protective guidelines."

The words leave her mouth based in legal truth, and that makes it totally believable. Ellie and Tick spent hours and hours at the local library studying federal land laws and creating legitimate appearing documents to prove what she says when the time comes.

Emory bites like a sucker fish because his ulterior motives always drive his personal needs, self-centered and egotistical. A true sociopath. Besides that, he'd love to bed Ellie and notch his belt one more time, another conquest. "So what's the problem?"

"We paid an upfront consulting fee to the assistant. She posts public auction notices, a legal requirement. Whenever she got a response, she wrote a postponement note to each party individually, but never officially filed a delay. We are the only bidder that knew the real date."

"In any other world than political that would be a bribe." Emory chuckles under his breath, admiring her ingenuity.

Ellie laughs with him, "Who cares, it's more like a little fudge on the table. Happens all the time. We coughed up the fifty grand and the greedy bitch wants it all. A bonus she calls it. But if the deal collapses, escrow returns it to us and she starts over, without us. Most legitimate bidders won't pay her the consult. We showed up alone, and bid it, escrowed the fifty grand. We got an option. We're in if we perform."

Ellie looks out the window, waiting for the question. Patience wins every time.

"Why would the deal collapse?"

"We have contingent private financing for all the development costs based on us acquiring the land title free and clear." She pauses, as if embarrassed or unsure whether she should share the next statements. Ellie inhales, a long deep breath and blows it out.

"I got in some trouble a while ago. A bit of creative financing for a few clients. The banks where we applied discovered a small manipulation of our data, and suspended my license. So, my initial bank funding for this purchase got denied, and the private development funding fails on this one unless we own a free and clear title."

"Creative financing?"

She explains in detail a method that bypasses basic qualifications and funds above equity loans on large developments and increases the loan to value calculation, a very sophisticated bending of the commercial mortgage rules. Something she and Tick fabricated in the library after reading a catalog full of banking law.

"I had no idea they'd suspend my broker license. The banks ran a background check and found it. Six months. We can't wait it out. Our contingency expires in four."

Emory grins. "I'm impressed. But you can't possibly believe that was legal. Of course they suspended you." Ellie just shrugs.

"That's falsified financing on your clients' purchase contracts." Emory laughs out loud. "A woman after my own heart."

"We can't do this one without the initial bank funding. The private investors don't believe we can pull this off against wilderness protection legislation until we own title. Once that happens, we get it all. Millions!"

Ellie sucks down her drink in one long swallow, and holds up her glass.

"Maybe I can help. Will you show me?"

Two more drinks arrive. She sits and stares at the ceiling, as if contemplating his request. Finally, "Wait here."

Ellie walks out to her car, retrieves the false drawings Tick and Frankie paid Benny Reed to produce, carries the package back inside, lays it out on the table. "Only reason I'm showing you, we own the option, otherwise, we'd keep it secret until we close the buy. You can't share with anyone."

Emory places a hand over his heart. "You have my word." He examines the development plot, the offices, the mall buildings, and an Urgent Care medical complex. He checks the new roadmap showing a four-lane highway exiting the interstate eighty miles away. "Very nice," he says. "Who would've thought?"

He stares at Ellie, engrossed in her as a woman, and admiring her as a potential business partner, the complete package. Infatuated. Obsessed. This bright and attractive woman and his first legitimate business deal in more years than he can count or remember, and right here in his palm at the same time. The initial Green Pastures development will come off completely legal, he believes, and Emory can hardly contain his glee.

"You really do your homework, don't you? How'd you find out about the new highway off the interstate?"

"I'm very good at my job."

Emory has no clue exactly how good.

* * *

Standing outside in the parking lot, Emory says, "Ride with me?"

"No thanks, I like my own wheels." Ellie aims the Jaguar at a large parcel of undeveloped land Tick and Frankie located on a map at the county land offices and scouted last week. Emory follows in the BMW. Forty minutes later, she pulls in off the highway above a large vacant parcel.

She climbs out and points, arching her hand across a wilderness area spreading out for miles. She convinced Emory she bought the inside track on a land purchase at a special closed bid auction. This land actually belongs to a joint venture trust between a non-profit wildlife preserve and the federal Bureau of Land Management, and can never be sold or developed.

"It's just this one, a fifty acre tract between the uplands and those three wet areas. That's why it works, it leaves the wetlands and scrub components. A little known law allows it. We discovered it, both the land and the law. We own a sixty-five acre parcel in Georgia, impossible to develop at any reasonable cost. It's nearly all floodplain. We trade, plus a half million in cash. Feds don't care. To them, it's just open land. To us, it's a fortune. We just need to match the appraisal, that's why the trade and cash."

Emory steps in behind Ellie and places a hand on each shoulder. Ellie fingers the small Buck knife in her pocket with which she cut Tank the night he assaulted Heath.

She releases the knife, spins easily out of his grasp and approaches the edge of a rock embankment overlooking the patch of wetlands and slightly rolling hills, partly forested and running off into the distance.

"Not now, Cal. I'm too tied up in this project. Perhaps later. Too much stress in my life now to enjoy a relationship."

The back of his head implodes almost as if he'd been hit with a baseball bat. Repeating itself over and over, the two-word phrase 'perhaps later' embeds in his brain.

Anything Emory can't have, he wants even more. The selfishness and financial independence he's experienced throughout most of his adult life denies him nothing, but this woman both excites him and pisses him off like no one he's ever met before. The fact he can't corral her simply intensifies his desire.

"Perhaps later," he repeats her casual remark aloud, a bare whisper no one hears but him. He rolls each word around on his tongue, savoring its taste, suddenly dizzy with lust.

Ellie stares into the distance as if she envisions the imaginary project springing to life right before her eyes. "It's right here," she points, "ready to rise up out of the earth."

In reality, she ignores the potential for development and appreciates the raw beauty of the land and its wildlife populations. She'd never touch this parcel with a shovel or a chainsaw, even if she owned it. Never.

Twice she pirouettes, a complete circle, her arms flying out to each side. She raises both fists in the air, embracing the sky. "Can you see it yet Cal?" Her eyes shine bright as stars, intensity radiates off her body, as if willing the birth of a building. "Can you?"

"I can," he says, staring out across the wetlands, bewitched. "I see it."

Ellie drops her arms and turns, gazing at Carlton Emory, her eyes wet with tears, the emotion nearly impossible to contain. Her act worthy of an Academy Award because in her heart Ellie McGee would rather cut his devious throat right here on the embankment and kick him over the edge.

Chapter Twenty-seven

Wednesday morning, Emory calls his attorney, then the bank, gets news that Steinmann set up and recorded the trust and the bank opened an account in the name of Richard Bailey as sole trustee.

He boots up his computer pulls up an international banking site and arranges a wire transfer for one million dollars into the trust, then another eight hundred thousand from a different source. One half hour later, he watches the trust account log in the funds, one million followed by the second deposit. "One point eight million." A grin splits his face as the words roll off his tongue.

Suddenly restless, agitated, he taps his fingers on the smooth, polished desk top, waiting for Ellie to arrive and discuss the auction deal again. Unwilling to commit his funding yet, she upped the stakes, promising she'd bring documentation he can review and authenticate in person.

Emory bit hard on her explanation yesterday, anxious to find solid ground since he lost his partners. He has no one to order around, except Harold, and the ex-cop has no clue how to perform business transactions.

Emory appears lost when nothing happens in his business life. He's always been a boss not a worker. He just gave orders and things happened. Not anymore.

He never meets his scam clients, never shows his face to anyone that can later identify him, a business decision he made early on to protect himself. He deals only with the funds, the money, and arranges the 'laundering service' so he can bank it and spend it. Money he understands, people not so much. His personality embraces the predatory aspects of social interaction. It's all he knows, all he's ever known, all he's ever cared about.

At age thirteen he cheated his younger brother out of the dollar they each made mowing a neighbor's lawn. He arm-wrestled him for it. His brother was nine, and smaller, much smaller. It launched his career as a devious, manipulating con man.

His sudden infatuation with Ellie, her bending the rules and her aggressive investment tactics combined with the threat of federal prosecution and failure stresses him out, leaves him with no mind of his own. He has no one to lead, so it becomes easy to guide him, and Ellie grabs that opportunity in both fists.

* * *

Ellie McGee crosses under the Green Pastures sign and pushes through the glass entrance doors, flashes her teeth. "Hello. You must be Harold. Mister Emory in?"

The security man nearly pops to attention in his seat. "Miss McPherson? Yes, go right on down. First door on the right. He's expecting you." Harold tips his cap then admires her walk as Ellie carries the development package with her along the corridor, knocks once, and steps inside the office.

Emory bounces up out of his chair and opens his arms. Ellie eludes the hug and offers a hand instead. "Business first, Cal." A firm, no-nonsense handshake backs him off. She lays out the series of false maps, fake building plans, and imaginary highway design. They examine the drawings, the plot plan, and contingency contract in detail.

"Look," she says, laying a series of documents Frankie and Tick copied and customized, closely duplicating the phony paperwork Emory used scamming Gina and Mickey McGee, but modified enough so he won't recognize it.

"This promissory note provides the percent of participation, and this portion," she points to a clause, "indicates the feds insure the deposit funds in this account until the deed records, so it can't default."

"Yes, I see it. A guarantee the funds are protected, insured by the FDIC."

Blinded by his desire, a low-cut top, skin tight clothing, and more gullible and less sophisticated than he believes of himself, Emory fails to recognize the doctored paperwork that his tech-smart partner created on the office computer and used to exploit his victims. He responds exactly as she'd hoped.

She nearly bursts out laughing. Under different circumstances, she might have done just that. Fooled by his own forgeries, an irony he absolutely deserves.

"Here we have the deed to our trade parcel in Georgia, sixty-five point three acres." She flips over another official document Frankie printed from the property appraiser's website in Folkston, Georgia. It's mostly flood land, and borders Okefenokee Swamp, a national wildlife refuge. She shows him several photographs Tick copied off a travel website.

Tick and Frankie duplicated the security documents and option pledges from the papers Cliff presented to Gina and Mickey McGee, changing only a few words and adding a gold embossed stamp Tick scanned off another page, along with some imaginary signatures and notary stamps, and a false auction agreement.

"We deposit the funds into an escrow, same as any other property transfer. If you want in, that's what it takes, Cal. We're in a hundred and seventy million dollar project here and the profit runs near thirty million. You're playing with the big boys now. We got extremely lucky with this find, almost an accident. It doesn't happen often."

"I feel a little uncomfortable with my money in another person's hands. It feels unsafe somehow, even if it's the feds." Always a relatively small time fraudster, Emory balks at the outlay of his capital. He wants it in a deposit account he can control. He never lets money out of his personal accounts into accounts he can't access.

"Feds won't allow that. The money goes to the legislative rep, she controls the funds until the feds record the titles, one from us to the feds, one from the feds to us, a mutual and simultaneous exchange of ownership, and the feds get the additional four hundred sixty three grand, the difference in appraised values."

Unsure of himself with no one to consult, he says, "I need to run this deal and this paperwork by my attorney."

"No dice. I'm keeping these documents right in my bag. I told you, this might not meet the legal expectations or requirements of ordinary property transfer, especially the federal government with that consult fee, the one you call a bribe. If you need anyone else to see these, especially personal attorneys, we withdraw. End of story, you're out."

She begins rolling up the drawings and stacking the documents. "Only reason you're in this at all, my license suspension cancels the bank funding. You came to me, remember? If we wait long enough, and pay a bit more consult fee, we get an extension and you're out anyway."

Ellie pauses her packing briefly, rolls her lip under her front teeth, gazes up at Emory as if contemplating him as a male she desires. "Besides, I like you Cal. Let's get this done now so we can relax together."

Emory slips in behind Ellie and tries again. He places a hand on her shoulder and slides a thumb onto her neck, an affectionate massage. "Please don't. Not yet Cal."

He takes that as progress, the not yet part, and continues rubbing her neck, starts massaging both shoulders. Moves in behind her a little closer.

Ellie reaches up, takes hold of an index finger at just exactly the right spot, and twists enough to hurt, just short of dislocation. A self-defense class for professional women she attended two nights a week during her college years pays off. "I said 'please' and 'don't' in the same sentence!"

Emory jerks his hand away and rubs his finger.

She turns her back on him, then very gently, over her shoulder, almost a whisper. "Once this is over, Cal, we can concentrate on our own pleasure. A getaway, an island somewhere, just the two of us."

She gathers her papers and exits into the corridor. Emery enjoys the view, a trim athletic figure and definite feminine sway. Assuming her comments 'perhaps later' earlier and 'not yet' now means he needs only a little more patience, a slick grin spreads across his face, he massages his finger again as the joint pain subsides.

"That bitch is gonna be so fucking worth it."

His imagination runs wild for a few egotistical minutes, basking in the gratification he expects and the selfishness he feels for himself. Emory rubs his crotch then quickly pulls his hand away as the door swings open beside him.

Ellie steps in empty-handed, pushes up on her toes, kisses Emory once, puts everything she has into it and seals his fate in that instant. He wraps his arms around her and pulls closer but she spins free, heads back out through the door, looks back over her shoulder and sends an unbelievably inviting and seductive smile his way.

"I'll call you tomorrow, you can let me know." She hurries along the corridor, grabs her package off the floor, runs outside, tosses the drawings and papers into the back seat, and hops into her car. Another Oscar level performance.

Half a mile down the road the bronze coupe slips onto a turn-out. The door kicks open. Ellie leans out and spits into the wind, a shudder runs down her body. She grabs a plastic bottle from her daypack between the seats, gargles, rinses her mouth out and spits again. She grabs a tissue, wipes her lips then takes another slug of minty mouthwash and spits one final time. "Blah! What a disgusting pig!"

Chapter Twenty-eight

Sitting at the table at home, drinking coffee the next afternoon, Emory remains undecided, holds back his decision, still unsure, with no one to confide in or ask advice. His phone dings. Ellie invites him to meet the rep, and the project supervisor, and her engineer at the site this afternoon. "Okay, two-thirty. Tight, but I'll get there if I leave right now...Yeah, I know the way."

* * *

Thirty-five minutes later, the sporty BMW eases in off the highway, parks on the embankment beside the Jaguar and the classic GMC pickup. Emory looks out the windshield, takes in the scene. Patches of melting snow highlight a diverse landscape.

Separated by lowlands and boggy terrain, two men crouch atop duplicate humps rising out of the wetlands fifty yards apart and both peer through scopes mounted on tripods. Clean shaven and professionally dressed, Tick and Frankie eyeball instruments and scream numbers back and forth. Each one scribbles a note when the other shouts. Annie and

Ellie stand side by side at the overlook, dressed like high-class professionals as well.

Amazing outfitters, local church thrift stores contain a variety of clothing and uniforms people donate from estates or just generally get tired of wearing, very inexpensive. Pick and choose can bring high quality to the table for a minimal cost.

Frankie wears a set of black eyeglass frames with clear lenses and performs exactly like the engineer he was educated to become, and was designated as during his initial commission in the Corps of Engineers. A high school and college athlete and very high energy, he found the dam building and water diversion less exciting, and volunteered for Special Forces, where he met Jake Klyne and thrived. He commanded the rescue squad that retrieved Ambassador Miller Winston when a drug cartel captured and imprisoned him in Panama several years ago.

Here and now, Frankie feels alive again, vibrant, working it like an operation, embedding in his personification as he'd done multiple times during his military career. Frankie loves the action, the front lines, feels right at home when emotions push adrenalin, even when it involves no true physical danger.

Emory watches Annie and Ellie. A discussion between the two women appears more like a disagreement, a little loud and argumentative. Annie looks over her shoulder as Emory exits his vehicle, and Emory listens as she speaks. "I don't like it, one more person we have to trust." He barely hears her words.

"It's the money man we need," Ellie responds quietly, nearly a whisper.

The shyster pretends he doesn't hear it, sidles up and sticks out his hand. "Carlton Emory," he says, "nice to meet you."

Annie ignores the hand, just long enough then shakes it roughly once and releases. "Annie Pitts."

Pinned to the outside of her jacket, an identification badge reveals her photo, her name, and Illinois Federal Legislative Assistant. A gold embossed state seal appears beneath her title and above a forged signature of the governor at the bottom.

Ellie explains, points out into the wetlands. "Our engineer and my project manager. Checking the corners, making sure we map exactly what we need. That parcel in the middle section needs to be directly in the center and dry or it won't pass the zoning. These guys have been at it since sunup this morning."

Tick pokes a fist in the air, Frankie the same. Frankie leans over and drives a wooden stake with a red flag into the ground. Both men start packing up the gear. The complete act required exactly one half hour out on the wetlands. Tick and Frankie deployed the equipment at two o'clock, the same time Ellie phoned Emory.

"Excellent! That flag marks the exact center of the new parcel we're creating. The zoning commission scheduled a special hearing tomorrow, just for this," Ellie says.

"Closed hearing, an 'executive session', the public can't attend." Ellie doesn't bat an eye telling the lie. She feels nothing at all for this crook, except disgust, fueled by the anger for what he did to her grandparents and other seniors she's never even met.

* * *

Unwilling yet to invest his money in the development, Emory makes his first appearance before the federal bench on the mortgage fraud cases the following Friday morning. He'd delayed his answer when Ellie pushed him a little, opting to wait until after this court hearing before he commits the investment funds. He sits beside Lester Steinmann and obeys the order, "All rise," when the judge enters.

Half an hour passes, filled with motions, arguments about funding, bank accounts, wire transfers out of the country, and a legal description of how this scam works. Federal prosecutor Colleen Barker, a young, newly anointed and relatively inexperienced assistant attorney general, presents an excellent case and describes the fraudulent documents and banking statements each victim submitted.

Judge Martin Sloan asks, "Opening, Mister Steinmann?"

"We waive."

She finally calls her first witness. "Leon Ingles."

Ingles inches his way his way up to the seat, leaning heavily on his cane. He wears an old double-breasted light green suit, a red tie, a red pocket handkerchief, and meticulously shined shoes. He struggles with seating himself, and finally looks up at the judge, then turns toward the prosecutor.

"He looks like a Christmas tree," Emory whispers. Steinmann ignores him.

Barker rolls through the introductions and finally says, "Mister Ingles, please explain how you and your wife became victims in this savings and mortgage fraud."

Ingles begins. "We met a man named John Reardon at a lunch our town library hosted. He claimed he was a private mortgage investor. Said he and his partner were project developers, and guaranteed eighteen percent on our money. We were only getting six percent at the bank on long-term certificates, so we decided it would benefit us. Triple interest."

"How did he convince you it was safe? How was your money protected?"

"Objection, your honor. Two questions."

"Sustained."

Barker aims a frown at Steinmann. "How did he convince you it was safe?

"He showed us a bunch of papers, all from the government he told us. Guarantees, and insurance certificates backed by the FDIC. It was all phony." His words reeked of bitterness.

"Did you do any other investigation of this company?"

"We looked at his website. It showed a lot of good reviews. The history goes back years. It showed other investments, other projects it developed, and some photos of large shopping centers and medical buildings he told us his company financed. We're not good at using the web, but it looked real to us."

A tear leaks out of his eye, he wipes it away. "It was all our savings, and he convinced us to mortgage our home. He stole that too." He glances over at his wife sitting on a wooden bench off to the side, wet streaks trickle down her cheeks. "We're living with our son now. All our hard work, all our retirement. Gone!"

"Do you see that man, John Reardon in this court today?"

"Leon stares directly at Carlton Emory, "No! But his boss is here." He points at Emory. "Right there!"

Steinmann pops to his feet. "Move to strike. Non-responsive."

"Sustained." He nods at the court reporter. "Ignore that accusation."

"Have you ever seen this defendant?" The prosecutor continues unabated.

"No, never. But he was part of it."

Steinmann half-rises and quickly objects again. "Move to strike the second sentence in his answer. Non-responsive." He resumes his seat.

"Sustained."

"No further questions, your honor."

"Your witness, Mister Steinmann."

Steinmann waves two photographs. "I have two photographs we obtained from the country coroner. We offer these as our defense exhibits one and two. Each of these men were identified as an accident victim a month or so ago." The attorney lifts another page, reads it and looks up. "November first and seventeenth. Both deceased."

"So accepted. Mark these one and two."

"May I approach the witness?"

"Approach."

Steinmann steps up to the witness chair, shows exhibit one. "Do you recognize the individual in this photograph?"

Leon says, "Yes. That's John Reardon."

"And, this one?"

"Yes. That's his partner, Cliff Porter, the mortgage guy."

"For clarification, your honor. Mister Ingles, have you ever seen the defendant, Carlton Emory? Yes or no, please."

Ingles stares across at Emory, says nothing.

Judge Martin Sloan says, "Mister Ingles?"

Ingles looks up at the judge, holds his answer a moment longer, then, "No."

"No further questions." Steinmann returns to his table.

The witness opens then shuts his mouth, obviously wanting to say more but can't. He pushes up onto his cane, totters over and slumps down beside his wife.

The remainder of the afternoon fills the time with six sets of witnesses. All claim similar fraudulent investments, submit similar documents, nearly identical except for the names and amounts. All six identify both photographs as the two men who led the fraud. None of the witnesses can identify Carlton Emory.

At three-thirty, Colleen Barker calls her final witness. Mickey McGee takes the stand. His glare nearly blows Carlton Emory backwards off his chair. Emory returns the stare, a slight upturn on his lips. None of these victims ever met him, a part of the personal strategy he designed to protect himself in exactly this situation.

The prosecutor begins, asking the same questions and receiving nearly identical responses. "Mister McGee, have you seen the man in this photograph?"

"Yes, John Reardon. He scammed us out of our savings."

"And, this one?"

"Yes. Cliff Porter. He's the partner. He did the mortgage fraud part."

"Do you see either one in this court today?"

Mickey McGee raises his eyebrows at the question. "No, you idiot. You know they're both dead!" McGee shakes his head in disgust and frustration. "No wonder you can't catch these guys!"

Judge Sloan bangs his gavel. "A little respect for the officers of this court, Mister McGee, or we'll remove you from this hearing and ban your testimony."

Barker gathers herself, blows out a breath and shakes her head, suddenly realizing how foolish her question was, and says, "Nothing further, your honor."

Steinmann approaches the witness, points at Emory. "Have you ever seen this defendant or heard the name Carlton Emory in association with any mortgage or investment, legal or otherwise, before today?"

Mickey McGee stares long and hard at Emory, "No, but I've talked to him on the phone."

"Move to strike," Steinmann snaps. "Non-responsive."

"Sustained."

Steinmann asks again, "Have you ever seen this defendant or heard his name before today? Yes or no only, please, Mister McGee."

McGee struggles with his answer, and finally says, "No."

'We're finished with this witness."

Colleen Barker stands. "The federal cases present as is, your honor. Mortgage fraud, six counts, and wire fraud, eleven counts. We have no further evidence or witnesses. The United States rests its cases."

"Very well. Mister Steinmann, your turn."

"We have one witness, your honor. Defense calls Doctor Damien Stokes."

The bailiff enters the courtroom accompanied by a short, round, middle-aged male dressed in an expensive blue suit. Damien Stokes takes the witness seat, pats his comb-over into place, and swears to tell the truth. Steinmann presents numerous credentials illustrating his witness qualifies as a hand-writing expert recognized in multiple federal and state jurisdictions.

"I have only one question. For your examination, we supplied a copy of each fraudulent document the prosecution submitted in this case. In your professional opinion, did Mister Carlton Emory sign any of these documents?"

"No. None of these documents bear his signature."

"Your witness, counselor."

"Mister Stokes ..."

Stokes interrupts, "It's Doctor Stokes."

"Sorry, Doctor Stokes. Is it possible the defendant altered his signature and changed his name, and signed any or all of these papers?"

"It's very unlikely. My colleagues and I examined the signature patterns extensively. As experts, we can usually find a tweak or twist that remains consistent even when a person intentionally creates a new signature."

Expecting a 'yes', her inexperience exhibits itself once more. Asking a question without knowing the answer undermines her attack. The answer pulls her lips down at the corners. She drops her eyes and stares at her feet. "Nothing further."

"Redirect?"

"Just one, our honor. How many experts reviewed these documents?"

"Three total. We have a four-partner consultancy, and we require at least three in agreement before we offer our opinion. In this case, it was unanimous."

"Thank you, Doctor." Steinmann opens his briefcase, withdraws a one-page document. He submits one copy to the court and one to the federal prosecutor.

"We hereby request Judge Martin Sloan consider a direct finding in this case due to lack of evidence and failure to identify the defendant as a participant in each fraud case before the bench on this date. His signature appears on none of the fraudulent exhibits as certified by Doctor Damien Stokes and his colleagues."

Judge Sloan agrees. "I need no time for consideration, the evidence is clear." He scribbles a few notes. "You're free to leave, Mister Emory. The federal custody motion is denied until the next show cause hearing. Make sure you appear."

"However, the assistant attorney general makes her case well enough and substantiates a connection between the money and the two deceased men. This district court will maintain custody of the accounts temporarily."

"Do you understand this ruling, and that you're required to appear again, Mister Emory, and you too counselor?"

He receives a 'Yes' from both men.

"Therefore, the freeze on funds remains in place for now. We'll address that again in two weeks on the eighteenth at nine o'clock in this hearing room." Sloan bangs his gavel, pushes out of his chair and exits, black robes swishing behind him.

"You win the first round, Lester," the federal prosecutor says, "but not the battle. We'll be back in two weeks." She gathers up her papers. "See you then."

"Nice to meet you too, Colleen." Steinmann smirks after her.

Red-faced and annoyed, Emory whispers to Steinmann. "What the fuck! What's he doing to me?"

"He made a ruling that keeps him in charge, Cal." The attorney slides papers into his briefcase and slams it shut. "It's not like you're broke and destitute. Have a little patience. A snap of his fingers won't get you out of this. You fucked it up, not me."

"If Martin released the funds, the FBI would appeal it overnight, and some court lackey would freeze it again anyway. And the feds could get Sloan removed for cause."

"Martin has to be very careful how he rules, and not blow it. At least he reversed the custody warrant, and keeps himself on the case, and you can leave, go home. Better than spending the next two weeks in a cell."

"Yeah, well Sloan won't get paid until I get my money. That goes for you too, Lester."

"Yeah, well, if you admit this money belongs to you and try to claim it, you might as well plead guilty and pack for Leavenworth at the same time. Save us another court date."

Emory slams his chair backwards and stomps out of the hearing room.

* * *

Saturday afternoon, Emory finds his regular bar stool at lunch time. Orders ham and cheese, and spicy fries. Sucks down a scotch, bangs the tumbler and pops a thumb up at Gordy. Five seconds later, a second scotch finds a home between his palms.

"Fuckin' court! The feds kept my money. They cheat!" He pours the drink down his throat in one long swallow then coughs. "Damn it, one more, Gordy." Emory chews on a few ice chips.

"Better slow down, you'll fall off that seat before you get the lunch plate." Gordy points a finger at the bar. "And, I'll take those keys again."

A ring tone begins, a shrill cartoon voice chirps, *Money, Money, Money.* Emory glances at the bar then pats his sports jacket, trying to find it. He hauls it out of a pocket, pokes it as the verse dribbles away, and barks into it. "Emory. What!"

The attitude falls away immediately. "Oh, hello Ellie. Sorry, thought you were someone else." He listens a minute. "Yeah, at EATS having lunch." Gordy sets a plate on the bar, a sandwich and fries.

"Come on over, I'm buying." He listens again. "You can't? You're meeting with the feds again." Ellie rambles on, explaining, commenting, convincing Emory it's time to choose. The conversation goes back and forth, Emory asking questions, then silence while he listens.

After fifteen minutes, he says, "Okay, I'm in, but will deposit my money only after the Zoning Board approval, and only if I can watch the account online ..."

"I know, I know, the feds won't let me sign on it, but I can watch it at least ... Okay, I'll meet you Monday here, at noon."

Chapter Twenty-nine

Annie pours her daily ration of morning coffee, filling a cup each for Tick, Ellie, Frankie, and Junkie, then empties the final drops into her own tin mug. She feeds a little more wood into the coals, and sticks another pot on to percolate.

"Emory wants to meet me at noon today," Ellie says. "I believe he's in, and will make a deposit today. He seems pretty antsy and needs money to live and function, and pay his legal fees. Based on what we know, what he told me, and what Scott wrote in an article he published this weekend, Emory may be short on funds."

"Judge Sloan vacated the arrest warrant, but left the federal hold active on the accounts. I know he has the cash somewhere, he already told me that, but he needs to earn for his future, and he'll never get back the fraud funds the feds confiscated. No chance of that no matter what he thinks."

Ellie and Frankie filed a business license last week in anticipation of opening a bank account to receive the funds. He tells Ellie, "Let the Captain handle this."

Ellie refuses. "Nope. I want personal control of the accounts Frankie, not an oak tree. As much as you believe the Captain will do a good job, we'll pass."

Frankie drives Ellie to Chicago and several international banks. They tried four banks before the new accounts representative accepted the license and the doctored identification they presented.

Ellie opens two new accounts, one savings and one checking. Frankie co-signs in case she gets in trouble with Emory and can't get to the bank if she needs it.

With the new banking laws in place, Frankie and Tick meticulously created false credentials at the library, then copied and laminated them at an office supply store.

She brought documentation and opened two bank accounts in the name of Broderick and Heath Engineering and Development. She and Frankie depart the final bank with temporary checks and a new savings account book in hand.

* * *

Sitting beside the burn barrel the next morning, Frankie tells everyone, "We just had to find a lazy bank clerk." He drains his cup and peeks in his hand, "Ready Captain?" Gets no response. Shrugs it off, wraps the red rag around his oak idol and replaces it in his jacket pocket.

"Let's go," he says and slides a camouflage wrap off his pickup.

Each time he returns from a drive, Frankie hides the pickup behind a thick stand of trees and under the tarp. No sense taking a chance that Emory may randomly drive past and expose the truck or the Jaguar. Little details like that might win or lose the game, and Frankie develops extremely thorough plans, even if he's still a little whacky inside his brain.

An operation gives him focus, and he occasionally shares the progress and their plans with Jake on late night phone calls in the privacy of his tent. Arnold and Sue let Ellie park the Jaguar inside the barn and protect it from the storms, according to what Ellie told them. The fewer folks that know the complete plan, the better and safer it is.

She hates lying to her friends, but told Arnold and Sue she inherited the Jaguar from an aunt and will likely sell it for travel money.

"Lucky gal," Arnold had said, and made her feel even worse. She told him she just wanted to protect it until she sold it.

Ellie hops into the passenger seat and Frankie engages four-wheel drive spins a few times in the snow, but eases the truck up over the embankment onto the highway. He drops Ellie off at the barn, returns, backs under the trees and tarps the truck again.

Frankie wanders over and salutes his tree, spots the sleek bronze Jaguar heading toward EATS, and the meeting between Ellie and Emory. "Okay, Captain. Looks like we're underway for real."

He squats down on his bedroll, removes his shoes and his foot, and begins his routine, a thrice daily workout. Up, down, up, down, up, down, his stump ankle lies atop his right calf. He counts the series when he exhales at the top of each pushup cycle, "One hundred." He flips over and begins sit-ups, finishes the count, installs his new foot and heads up onto the highway for a ten-mile jog. His new foot fits like a warm mitten and carries a smile with it every time he runs.

* * *

After days of discussion, disagreement, promises, threats, and at least one compromise, Emory finally signed the investment deal, and told Ellie he'd wire the money into the federal escrow account.

At first, Emory refused unless he could access the account balance online. Ellie told him that's not legal. The feds won't allow anyone but the registered legislative assistant he met to disburse the funds. He insisted though, that once he transfers the deposits, he must have at least access to watch it.

Ellie agreed, gave him a 'visual only' password she contrived with the bank manager, telling him she was teaching her young son about bank accounts. She wants him to see it, but be unable to cash anything out. The branch manager set it up as a private trust, trustee access only, but visual online to anyone with a pass code.

He told her, 'Never can start too early teaching our children financial responsibility,' and following that comment, she left the man with a smile on his face.

* * *

Sitting across from Emory in the booth at EATS, she hands him a deposit slip with the account number on it. "Make this today, or the trade-purchase may not close in two days. Apparently, another developer got wind of this swap and it's trying to interfere. Some financial group out of Denver might make a higher offer, and they have a more valuable parcel to trade."

In her one not so smart decision, she expresses her lack of knowledge about banks, and never thinks about the possibility of security issues with large deposits or transfers due to banking laws. She sticks the signed documents in her briefcase, slides out of the booth, and departs. Emory watches the Jaguar back out and disappear down the highway.

Emory drops his forehead down on his palms, as if contemplating the enormous risk he's about to take. He hates losing control of nearly a third of his bankroll, especially after the FBI froze a big chunk of his dollars. He's always been the money man in his fraudulent operations.

"The cost of going legit," he mutters, "may be too high."

He blows out a long breath, opens his laptop and logs in, calls up his bank website, enters his password, hesitates another minute, shakes his head and closes out the website. He stares out at the parking lot for ten minutes.

Emory opens his laptop again, logs in, keys in his code and the amount, four hundred sixty-five thousand and ninety dollars. He holds his finger in the air, counts to ten under his breath, hits the transfer key, shuts the laptop, and carries it over to his corner stool.

"Gimme a double, Gordy. I really need this one."

His ring tone kicks into its cartoon lyric. He snatches if off the bar after the second '*Money*' squeaks out. "Emory." He listens, hesitates briefly, then, "Yes, Allen. That's correct. Clear the wire transfer under my authority. Thanks for verifying." He shuts the phone.

After a couple minutes and two doubles, he logs into the false escrow account where Ellie promised him his money will sit until the closing, the day after tomorrow. Every thirty seconds for nearly an hour, he peeks at the account. Every six minutes the online security kicks him off the site for lack of activity. He logs back in, cursing the bank and the feds each time.

Finally the funds hit. Four hundred sixty-five thousand and ninety dollars magically appear, and add to the initial one hundred dollar deposit. He logs in every fifteen minutes thereafter, checking the balance, afraid his money might disappear.

The stress and worry gives him a headache, assisted by more scotch over ice. Each time, the same figure greets his inquiry and the headache disappears. Fifteen minutes later it's back, and he logs in again. The scotch and his watchdog behavior drag late into the evening until Gordy grabs his keys and orders Emory the only cab in town.

* * *

At eleven forty, twenty minutes before the security system triggers its daily large transaction warnings at midnight, Frankie dusts the snow off a log outside his tent, sits, and dials a series of numbers, then hangs up.

A minute rolls by, his phone dings once. He flips it open. "Yeah, the funds hit today." He listens a few seconds. "No, Captain didn't tell her. He was afraid she wouldn't go for it and if she didn't agree, Captain had no time to convince her or create and alternate sequence."

Frankie listens again. "Okay, four minutes and it's a done deal. Will explain it tomorrow morning." He flips the phone shut, crawls back into his tent.

* * *

Alone, Ellie creeps out of the dual cubby in the pitch dark of early morning. She climbs up onto the highway, hitching a ride into town. Arnold picks her up just as they planned yesterday. She hops into the cab and Arnold heads into town just as the sun arcs its early morning rays above the horizon. He drops Ellie at the bank.

"Pick you up here in an hour, Ellie." He heads on over to buy vitamins, feed supplements, and a new water hose.

Awake finally at ten minutes past eight and sporting an exceptionally aggressive hangover, Emory opens the account and stares at a zero balance. At first disbelieving his eyes, he logs out and logs in again. Then the fury takes over. He slams the laptop shut, dials the bank. The manager refuses him any information due to federal banking regulations and security issues.

He screams into the phone, recites the account number.

"We can't talk about an account you don't sign on."

"I can sign in, I can log in. Here's my password." Emory almost begs.

"Sorry sir, that password shows invalid."

"Try it again." He raises his voice again, more demanding this time.

"We just did, three times. No change. Sorry we can't help you."

The phone clicks in his ear. Emory glares at the dial face and pitches the phone across the room. It shatters against the wall. He slouches down at the kitchen table, wraps his arms around himself, and rocks back and forth. "Fuck. Fuck. Fuck! That bitch! What has she done to me?"

Suddenly he runs outside, hops in the black BMW this time and swings up onto the highway. Red-faced and speeding toward the bank, his temper flares, sweat pours off his body and soaks into his shirt. "Fuck, fuck, fuck," he grunts, "Must be a mistake. Must be a mistake!" Easing up only slightly at the crosswalks, he runs two red lights on the way to the bank, and ignores several four-corner stop signs as if they don't exist.

* * *

As usual, the smell of coffee and burning pine boughs greets the remaining camp occupants. Frankie exits his tent, clears a spot in the inch or two of icy fluff that fell overnight, lays his long coat on the ground, and begins his pushup count. His empty left pant cuff lies across his right calf, his standard workout form.

Rising later than usual today and well past sunrise, Junkie parks himself on a stump beside Annie and sips his first cup of the day. Both heads and eyes rotate in tandem toward the rattle trap pickup wheeling into the gravel turnout.

Arnold brakes to a stop and Ellie jumps out, slams the door, slips and tumbles down the embankment. She pops up, aims a hundred ten pounds of fury directly at the oak tree and stomps across the camp toward Frankie, face as red as a cherry, and fists and knees pumping hard. Tears fill her eyes and spill over.

Pushing himself upright and balancing on his foot, Frankie watches her side step past the burn barrel, coming fast. The entire city of Chicago probably hears the slap as her right palm connects with his left cheek. She punches him on the chest, again and again, pouring her rage into every blow. Solid as a rock, Frankie absorbs the blows easily, while Ellie vents her anger.

"Where is it, Frankie? Where is it? There's only eighteen thousand in the savings, and a dollar in the checking!" She pummels his arms and chest, kicks him again and again.

He blocks a second slap, and easily gains control. Extremely well-trained and much stronger than Ellie, Frankie grabs her wrists, spins her in place and pulls her shoulders into his chest. He embraces her completely while she struggles, and flips himself backwards into a snow bank. Ellie lands on his chest.

He swings a calf over each ankle, pinning her atop his body, and both lie entwined in the snow until Ellie quits struggling. After another long minute, she runs out of breath and energy. Frankie keeps the pin in place, holding Ellie motionless.

"You done yet?"

"No! Never!" She puts all her strength into it, kicks and squirms for another minute to no avail, then gives up and lies still, sucking in wind.

"Tell your fucking big-shot Captain Woody over there I want that money back, Frankie! Today. NOW!"

Ellie starts kicking and bucking again, tears streaming down her cheeks.

Frankie immobilizes Ellie until she wears herself out. "You done yet?" Frankie asks again. Gets no response. Another useless kick and twist fails.

Junkie yells, "Hey, what's going on over here?"

Approaching slowly, Annie and Junkie wonder what happened to bring on such anger, and want to help or interfere, depending on the answer. Awakened by the noise, Tick crawls out of the cubby and observes the scuffle momentarily, puzzled and half awake. He stumbles toward Frankie, aiming to protect Ellie regardless of the reasons.

Frankie barks at Tick. "Don't!" Still confused, Ticks stops in his tracks.

"I'm gonna release your left arm, Ellie. Take this and dial your Granny," Frankie orders, and offers her his burner phone, "Here, take it. Call your Granny. Put it on speaker, so we all hear it." The Captain Cooper command tone in his voice freezes everyone in place, including Ellie. Her anger temporarily spent, she thumbs in the numbers one-handed, and fires up the speaker.

Her grandmother answers on the first ring, and Ellie says, "It's me!"

Granny interrupts. "Ellie! It's a miracle, Ellie. We got a call from Horace Greenleaf today, at our bank, at eight-fifteen this morning. We got all the money back. It's all there, plus some interest."

"What? What do you mean ... 'You got all the money back' ... how?"

"An overnight wire came in according to Horace, came from offshore somewhere. He says it's what the bank calls 'a clean, no trace wire' and deposited a total of four hundred forty-seven thousand and eighty four dollars. That's more than we lost. So, interest."

"Where did it come from? How?"

"He doesn't know. A cash wire came in to our account, directed to Gina and Mickey McGee, to both of us. Into our savings. It's been our account for years, ever since we got married." Easy to read her mood over the speaker, Granny practically bleeds jubilation right through the speaker.

The McGee retirement life restored itself overnight and the happiness bubbles over. She can't help it. "We tried to call you, but we have no number for you. We'll buy you a phone, Ellie." Her Granny smile nearly transmits itself right over the lines.

"I'll call you back, Granny."

She flips the phone shut, tosses it aside. Still lying in the snow beneath Ellie, Frankie says, "Okay, you now know." He releases her hands, and untangles his legs.

"Captain fixed it. Told you he would."

Ellie rolls off Frankie and Annie helps her to her feet. Junkie offers a hand and Frankie swings up on his right foot beside her. Both dust off the ice crystals.

One final punch with minimal power behind it hits Frankie in the chest. "Why didn't you tell me?"

"Can't. Captain told me not to tell anyone. You're anyone, too."

Another punch lands on his chest, lighter still, then Ellie wraps both arms around him in a bear hug, sobbing, discharging all the pent-up stress. Suddenly unable to catch her breath, she sobs again and again, more tears stream down her cheeks, this time for a different reason, joy not anger. Frankie returns the hug, his muscular arms pulling Ellie in close now, sharing the powerful emotions.

"I'm sorry Frankie. You're my friend, and I didn't trust you. The money gone again scared me."

"I know." He responds softly and releases her, draws back a few feet. "I know."

Frankie wrinkles his nose. "Damn, you need a bath, Ellie!" Looks down at himself. "Oops, guess that's me." He glances over his shoulder. "Right Captain?"

"So, what's with the eighteen grand? And, how'd you do it?"

"Captain ain't telling. Your Granny and Gramps got their share. The rest pays back expenses. You got investors here, remember? Your friends."

"More like family." Ellie holds out both arms. All five wrap up in the emotion of the moment. The struggles and the tragedy that gripped their lives the past two months releases all at once. Annie squeals, "We did it!" Raises both fists in the air and dances in a circle. "We did it!"

His lips tip up at the ends, barely. Frankie reaches into his jacket, pets the oak stub and whispers, "Thanks Captain." No one else hears. "And thank the Senator next time you see him. Tell him the job's almost done."

Annie says, "This calls for some coffee, with a party spike in it."

Frankie takes a few steps backward and drops down on his long coat, picks up the count exactly where Ellie interrupted. Begins his pushup count at fifty-six. "Be there in a few minutes. Don't empty that jug without us."

* * *

A Fed-Ex delivery truck rolls into the gravel turnout above the culvert. The driver waves, and stumbles his way down the slope carrying a large envelope. He reads the label, looks around the camp. "Eleanor McGee here?"

Ellie raises her hand. "Sign here." The driver hands her the envelope then laughs. "Never done this before ... A hobo camp."

"We're vagabonds," Annie corrects him.

The package contains a certified document originating at Shady Oaks Investments, an account once owned and operated by Cliff Porter and John Reardon, and a man named Jason Mitchell. The balance sheet shows one deposit minus a hundred and fifty dollar wire service fee, waived.

"Mitchell," Ellie says. "That's the telephone guy, we never met him. He just gave us instructions over the phone."

A wire record shows the balance at zero, in and out deposit funds, service fees, and transfer amounts, and the receiving account in the name of Gina and Mickey McGee. An accompanying document illustrates a refund balance sheet from Shady Oaks Investment account, the fraudulent company that scammed Gina and Mickey McGee. The account had been closed several years ago.

The routing sheet indicates the Shady Oaks account re-opened for one day, accepted the funds from an indefinable source offshore, wired the funds through an untraceable intermediate financial company based in Switzerland, and closed again the same day. It lists a single transaction, a payout for the initial McGee investment plus interest, minus processing and document fees. No further explanation.

The certified paperwork serves as proof that the Gina and Mickey can claim the money legally, with no recourse from the Internal Revenue Service or the federal banking investigators. They legally owned and invested the money at one point, so the papers simply show a return of capital, routed thru an offshore investment firm, back-dated, and wired into their private account. Almost completely legal, but they don't know the difference, and bask in their good fortune.

* * *

Brenda Davis sits alone with her regional supervisor in a meeting room. "Once we bring Emory in again, we'll sweat it out of him. Emily's writing up the new arrest warrant as we speak. Brandon Marks will sign it immediately. We know most of the victims, we'll find the rest, and the court already appointed a trustee to divide the spoils." She slides a file across. "We'll share the file with SEC and DOJ whenever we're done. They'll take over."

"We haven't located Emory yet, but we will. He can't get away, and he's got no money. At least none we know about."

Based on the FBI records, most victims will get back a pretty good portion of what they lost, at least sixty or seventy percent once a court-appointed receiver recovers the funds, plus all the interest it generated while it sat there idle. Most fraud recoveries end up paying out pennies on the dollar, so the investors got lucky with this one.

Emory was saving it for his retirement instead of wild spending like most of these fraud managers. The SEC will sell the townhouse he owns downtown, worth one million six-hundred thousand and no mortgage, one silver BMW 335i and one black BMW 535i, and the office complex worth seven hundred fifty thousand, at least. No mortgage there either. The furnishings in his townhouse and the rental condo cost well over a hundred grand. The fancy desk in his office, eight grand alone.

"Expensive taste these crooks develop, especially with other folks' money." Brenda says. A satisfied grin slips onto her face, as she contemplates a trial and a guilty verdict, but for more than any other reason, this time she got the money back and can repay most of the senior citizens Emory and his crew ripped off.

"We got him, finally. Froze his bank accounts and the fake trust. Got Steinmann too, and that rat fink Martin Sloan as well, a federal judge no less, and will grab any mystery accounts Steinmann and Sloan own soon as we find them. We're looking now, got the warrant signed this morning."

Brenda flips open the folder and runs her finger down a column. "Got every dollar, just under two and a half million total. Well, almost all. Seems Emory got away with just over four hundred sixty three thousand somehow, we can't find yet. Maybe never will."

"That's not counting Steinmann and Sloan. We'll tag their private accounts and get that money too. We don't have a total of everything they got paid, but once we do, it looks like most of the victims will get back a pretty good chunk of what they lost."

"And, Hargrove arrested Harold Bunny yesterday. He's squealing like a stuck pig, willing to rat everything off for a deal. We might not need him, if we don't, we'll cook him up right alongside the others."

* * *

Ellie and Tick sit in a booth at EATS, poking at a late night snack, drinking coffee, complaining about the lack of progress with prosecutions. Ellie's not satisfied that Emory runs free, but she can't offer any evidence without implicating herself and her friends in the game they all played. Tick grunts his disgust as well. "He sent the guys to beat my brother. We know it, just can't prove it."

"The judge cut Emory loose again. Another technicality of some sort. Even after the security guy spelled everything out, and they let him go too, for now at least."

Gina and Mickey used some of the money, hired an attorney and sued Emory, joining with a few others in a mini-class action. "Can't imagine how he keeps winning in court. Every time, it's like he carries the judge on his payroll." More truth in that statement than Tick or Ellie know.

"Granny says she'll never give up, Gramps too."

"Emory sent those three thugs after my brother, makes him guilty no matter what the law says!" The loss shows clearly in his words, his eyes bleed tears and his words emerge deep and angry with a promise.

"I'm gonna find that bastard! No way I'm letting this go, legal or not. If the feds don't bust him first, I'll put him in a grave myself!"

* * *

The assistant knocks on the door once, sticks his head in and says, "They're here." He pushes the door open, stand aside, and waves in Scott Monroe and Joe Eagleton.

Brenda Davis greets the reporter and the deputy, thanks each for his insights, and the leads both put together and shared. "It really helped my squad see a bigger picture. You go after things we don't or can't. We focus on one component, and have federal jurisdiction issues that occasionally get in the way of progress."

Davis encapsulates and updates. "We froze that new trust today, it's phony anyway. He's cooked, and we'll burn him to a crisp this time. We'll repay his victims, and, once we find him, Mister Carlton Emory will grow a lot older and a lot grayer before he sees the free side of cell bars again."

Investigative records show some of the folks he ripped off also identified the photos of his dead partners. His ex-cop security guy can't wait to cut a deal and rat on the fraud scheme and the money laundry. The FBI found accounting legends and names of the victims on a flash drive taped beneath a drawer in the old abandoned offices.

"That Patterson slash Porter guy saved the digital records and taped a disk under his old table in the abandoned offices they vacated before he sailed off that bridge. The feds didn't hold Bunny today, but he's dealing and squealing. No ex-cop wants to see the inside of a prison. "

The marshals applied for a new warrant and will arrest Bunny again. Eventually, the victims should get at least some or most of the investment funds back. Anything's better than shooting a blank in this case. Most of the folks that get scammed never get the money back. Emory's one very smooth character, but very nasty as well.

"We got lucky, froze his money before he could move it. He disappeared again, but we have a lead. He won't get away." Davis hopes she's right, but at the moment the feds have no leads. Emory disappeared off the face of the earth.

"That's about it for now guys. We thank you for all your help, Scott, and you too, Joe. It brought these guys down a lot quicker than we would have otherwise."

* * *

Miller Winston drops into his favorite lounge chair overlooking Barnstable Harbor and flips open his phone. "Thanks, Vicki. Put it through." He hits the speaker button and lies back, links his hands behind his head, relaxing. "What have you got for me, Mister White?"

A voice squeaks over the speakers. "Regarding the audit you asked about? Our search engines tick a prowler box and then call a human when it finds something odd in an investment account," the IRS flunky says. "That's why we looked at that deposit into the McGee account, just under four hundred fifty grand, pretty big chunk of money."

"Right. It's legitimate cash from an investment instrument. Retirement dollars funded it. They put the money in, now they want it back. So What?"

"It appeared a bit shaky, so the robot caught it and kicked it up to us. Now that you've explained it, Senator, it makes sense. First live glance, it looks okay. We'll just sign off on it and file it. Just a little odd, so we took a peek."

"Seems like the IRS has better things to spend it's time on, Mister White. They're retired farmers, seniors, solid Americans. Leave it alone and find something worth your time."

"Yes sir. Consider it done."

* * *

"You like this headline, Matt?" Scott Monroe reads it to his boss. "Seniors Invest in Fraud," then the sub-head, "Local FBI busts small-time hood and federal judge in big bucks financial scam."

"Got any art?"

Scott pops two thumbs up, drops three photos on the desk. One shows Emory leaving his offices, alone. One shows Judge Sloan at a fancy awards dinner. The last one shows an attractive FBI agent leading Emory into the courthouse, in handcuffs. He's gone again though. Judge released him one more time just before Davis arrested Sloan and Steinmann.

"That's Brenda Davis, leading Emory in last week. She getting new warrants, and will chase him down again soon as the magistrate signs off and files it."

Hoffman nods his approval, "Yes, I remember her." He winks at Scott. "Hard to forget. She has no leads yet? Emory's still hiding out?"

"Yup, nothing. Like a fox in a hole."

Scott pulls up the full article on his laptop, reads it along with Matt.

Chicago ex-cop Harold Bunny spills the beans to avoid federal and state agencies stacking charges against him. Bunny, a one-time Chicago police officer fired for blackmailing drug dealers and prostitutes ten years ago, was arrested in an investment fraud scheme that claimed millions in retirement savings and phony mortgages. Bunny served as a security officer in the fraudulent investment company.

Wheeling and dealing for a lighter sentence, Bunny alleges his boss and two deceased partners ran the scam on seniors for several years in numerous mid-west areas, absconding with the funds and changing identities each time the investigators followed up on complaints.

Deputy Joe Eagleton states the two partners died in separate accidents, but under odd conditions. The homicide investigation remains open and the coroner's office will continue evaluating evidence. Despite extenuating circumstances in both deaths, the county coroner predicts he will close out the cases as alcohol induced accidents unless he finds more evidence.

FBI Agent Brenda Davis, a financial crimes investigator and district supervisor, said, "Our office located and froze nearly two and a half million dollars in three accounts belonging to Carlton Emory, the alleged ringleader."

Nearly half a million dollars remains unaccounted for, and disappeared a week ago into an offshore banking system. The FBI continues tracking the money, but tells Bank Notes the funds seem to have vanished into a vacuum.

Davis served federal arrest warrants today on Lester Steinmann, a local attorney that assisted in the scams, and Martin Sloan, a federal judge, for soliciting and accepting bribes and payoffs in the schemes and illegally ruling on motions to prevent or delay prosecutions. The FBI continues its investigation and expects to recover more investors' money when it confiscates accounts in the names of Steinmann and Sloan.

Davis said. "My agents are attempting to locate Emory now. He paid a ten thousand dollar bond in court this morning Judge Martin Sloan set just two hours before FBI agents arrested Sloan for participating in the financial fraud cases."

"District Judge Sandra Morrison vacated that bond a half hour ago, and signed a new arrest warrant for Carlton Emory. We'll take him into custody soon as we find him," Davis advised the Bank Notes investigator.

Steinmann and Sloan deny any involvement and remain in custody, but Bunny alleges both men assisted Emory in fraudulent activities extensively over the past several years. Bunny was released on his own recognizance this afternoon, but continues to work with FBI agents and the local authorities.

Agent Davis said, "Harold Bunny's singing like a sparrow on a feeder."

Hoffman says, "Nice job, Scott. A real ball-buster. Gets you a bonus, too."

Scott bumps fists with his boss, spins in a circle, grins, and taps his wallet, then whips out his assignment book. "I'm ready! What's next on our agenda?"

"Keep your finger in this Emory pie as it plays out. But here, take this. Got a tip from our buddy, Banker Ben. Might have a couple washing drug money though a Laundromat. If that don't tickle your ironic button, nothing will.

Hoffman laughs, tosses a file folder across the desk. "Here, take a peek. The building's over in the Pickering District. Can't imagine sixty grand a month coming through any business in that rat-hole."

Chapter Thirty

Carlton Emory bypasses the front entrance and glances at the security kiosk inside. Empty booth, no Harold.

"Probably masturbating in the men's room," Emory mutters.

He swings into his parking slot at the rear, shuts off a rented Ford. An unlit corridor and a dim office greet him. He unlocks his private door and flips the switch. Nothing, overhead lights remain dark.

Emory shrugs. "Fuckin' maintenance."

Streetlights along the road provide a dim light through his rear windows. He works his way across to the wet bar, pours himself a Cognac, then pulls out an antique leather chair and sits at his desk, sips, stretches, sips again, rolling the sweet fruity liqueur around on his tongue. The fingers on his right hand tattoo a rhythm on the expensive Rosewood desktop. A smile crosses his face. "They've got nothing yet, except my cars."

"Nice job today, Martin," he whispers, reflecting upon the motion and bond Judge Sloan granted earlier, about two hours before the feds arrested him. A third court delay today pleases Emory immensely, and more coming. He believes it will be years before the cases actually settle, and a trial takes even longer. If he loses, he'll just fold the company and vanish again. Not for the first time either. He's already making plans.

He has no idea Sloan and Steinmann have already been detained without bail earlier today. No idea that all his accounts have been frozen again. No idea Brenda Davis awaits a new arrest warrant and will serve it as soon as it's filed. In fact, he's not hiding, but the legal paperwork takes forever and the timing never makes sense, so Emory sits and waits with no knowledge about the pending arrest.

A frown suddenly wipes out his grin. "I'll get that bitch. No one fucks with me! And no one steals my money." He growls into the ice as he tips up his drink.

Emory boots up his laptop, and begins a log-in sequence and prepares to move the remaining money he thinks is still accessible in his accounts, has no idea the feds already froze it.

A vehicle swings the curve outside, then a second behind it. Each one briefly shines its headlights in through the window and blinks across a shadow standing near the entry then passes on, leaving the room in semi-darkness again.

Startled, Emory barks, "Who the fuck're you?"

"Captain Frank Cooper."

Emory tilts his head, tries to get a good look at his intruder. "So?"

Captain Cooper points a finger at the ceiling. "Lights don't work."

Emory shuts his laptop, pulls the gold chain on an antique green-glass desk lamp. This one flicks on, revealing three fluorescent light bulbs lying across the desk and a dark human form wearing an old military long-coat over clean, pressed fatigues. A camouflage cap and neatly trimmed whiskers obscure his face. Emory looks up at the empty ceiling fixtures, then back at the stranger, then again at the light bulbs on his desk.

"Get the hell out of here before I call security." Emory grabs the phone, punches a speed dial and listens. Nothing. Hollow emptiness echoes back into his ear. He glances at the phone briefly, drops it back into its cradle.

"Ain't no security." The Special Forces veteran takes two steps closer into the light, tilts his head, nearly revealing his face. "Phone don't work, alarm button on the floor don't work neither."

Emory moves his foot, glances down at the silver activator button beneath his desk, opens a drawer and wiggles his hand around inside then reaches in a bit deeper.

"Looking for this." Captain Cooper eases his left hand out of his coat pocket, casually points the barrel of a Glock 23 at the floor. "Just need a minute of your time, that's all. Shouldn't have done what you did. Heath was my friend."

"Who the fuck's Heath?" Emory pushes out a bit of arrogance, always believes he's in control. That he can buy anything or anyone, just negotiate a price.

"Nobody now. He died."

"What's that got to do with me?"

"You sent the men who hit him down at the camp."

Awareness blinks on inside his warped, selfish brain. "We didn't mean that. Just wanted to scare him, an accident." As if calling the violent death of an innocent man an accident makes it okay, as if it relieves Emory and his flunkies of all responsibility.

Captain Cooper says nothing.

"What do you want? Money?"

"Nope. Got a foot first. Don't need money."

Puzzled by the comment, Emory asks, "So, what do you want, why're you here?"

"Want? Nothing. You should know why though. Fair's fair."

Confused Emory asks, "Why what? What's fair?"

Captain Cooper locks eyes with Emory.

Emory shrugs, but curiosity wins. "Ok, I'll bite. Why?"

"Heath. Ellie. Tick. Gina and Mickey McGee."

Emory spreads his hands wide, as if puzzled or mutely questioning. Then the names Gina and Mickey McGee register in his mind. "The McGees?"

Frankie nods his head. "Yup. Ellie McGee. Ain't no Ellie McPherson. She's the grand-daughter. That real estate deal? She tricked you, took the money back."

Emory stares at the intruder, still puzzled. He's not quite put the entire package together yet. Captain Cooper steps closer, lifts his head slightly, the brim of his cap no longer shields his face. Emory's eyes pop wide open as the revelation hits home and suddenly he knows. "You! You're the surveyor, the engineer."

Emory throws his drink across the room. The glass shatters against the wall. His cheeks turn crimson when he figures it out. Enraged, he thrusts himself up out of his chair, his rage emerging.

"Ellie McGee? He barks out the question, though the answer flashes across his mind before he even asks it. "This whole setup was a scam!"

"Yup." The Glock 23 holds thirteen rounds. A Special Forces soldier only needs one. Indoors, the pop sounds a bit louder than this Glock normally makes at an outdoor range. The windows vibrate slightly in the enclosed space. Late at night, an empty office building, no security, no one hears it.

Both his eyes bulge out and roll upwards as if examining the wet red dot that appears in the middle of his forehead. The back of his head explodes. The slug punches through a single glass pane and spins off into the weeds. His final thought seeks some rationale for an extremely sharp pain Emory feels for one infinitesimal fraction of a second while his nerves quiver and shake, and his brain shuts down.

An oddity in and of itself, the last word Emory spoke in his life was 'scam'.

His bladder empties. His thigh muscles kick out, a reflex action, and the fancy leather chair rolls back, hits the wall then tips forward. Carlton Emory falls on his face.

"Meant that one Cal. Ain't just trying to scare you."

Frankie collects the ejected shell, flips over a glass tumbler and pours a Cognac, neat, sucks it down in one long gulp, and sticks the casing and the bottle in his pocket.

He releases the clip, empties the remaining rounds into his pocket, slides the empty clip back in the slot, unwraps his handkerchief, holds the oak stub up in front of his eyes. "Cliff knew it, Captain. So did John, right there at the end before his head hit the tub," he tells the oak stub face. "Told 'em both. Fair's fair."

Frankie wraps the handkerchief around the idol, sticks it back in his pocket. He spins a crisp about-face and marches out into the hallway, no limp.

A few thumps echo in the corridor, Harold banging on the closet door. Frankie grins. "Have a nice night, Harold. Feds are coming for you tomorrow. You're cooked."

Frankie angles across the parking lot and picks up a gravel path edging the highway, begins the six-mile trek along the road then through the woods back toward the hobo camp. Three times he ducks into the brush when a vehicle appears and lights up the pavement. A mile out he slips unseen into the forest.

Captain Cooper dismantles the Glock as he goes, randomly burying a piece here and a piece there, each one a few inches deep beneath the brush. Three miles in, he grabs a rock, smashes the casing flat and buries it in the woods too. Saves the gloves for the burn barrel later. He jogs the remaining three miles on his brand new prosthetic foot, no problems and no discomfort, nice fit.

Frankie can now enjoy an exercise that's been missing in his life for several years. A track star in high school and college, Frankie loves running.

"Don't hurt, got a foot first."

Chapter Thirty-one

Senator Miller Winston makes a second call. The IRS inquiries short-circuit and shut down. The tax investigation aimed at Gina and Mickey McGee and a separate investigation questioning the expense repayment money that suddenly appears in an account Annie Pitts controls vanish into a locked file cabinet. The records simply disappear into the same financial vacuum that generated the funds initially.

Annie divides the funds according to the original group agreement and closes the account she never actually opened.

Two days later, unbeknownst to the players, every bank account associated with the hobo investment game evaporates. No record of the closed accounts remains, not even on backup disks, and the filed documents disappear from a locked cabinet drawer.

Gina and Mickey McGee have no clue how the strange investment fraud resolved itself but looked into a nice townhouse overlooking a small pond on the outskirts of Chicago. They enjoy the newly refunded retirement and ask no questions.

Ellie quietly and sincerely expresses her gratitude, absolutely certain Jake and Frankie assisted behind the scenes. "I know you helped all this happen, I don't know how, and don't care, but thank you Frankie. And my family thanks you too, you and Jake, wherever he is."

Captain Frank Cooper supplies a knowledgeable grin, but admits nothing. She parks the information in the back of her mind forever. Frankie turns away, marches back and salutes his tree, then drops down onto his fingertips and begins a count.

* * *

As the night consumes the last remaining daylight, Tick and Ellie lie side by side on a pair of sleeping bags inside the raggedy brush cubby, both staring out through the entry arch and watch the burn barrel flare up into the dusk. Tick slants his eyes sideways, peeks at Ellie. Installs a puzzled look on his face, unsure of the future.

"Think we should head for California or Oregon?" Ellie asks. "Getting tired of the cold here. Nothing keeping us here now. Can always come back and visit."

"We? ... Us?"

"You been looking, watching, staring. I'm just lying here wondering when you'll be touching."

"You belonged to my brother, not me. That means something."

"Don't belong to anyone, just me. We met up, traveled together, no commitment. We enjoyed the company. I miss him, like a pal, like a friend with benefits. I'd miss you different if you disappeared. We're a team now."

"I'd never trespass, but my brother's gone now. Feels like half of me went with him."

"I know, twins in appearance, but something missing in Heath I find in you, Tick. Heath was a traveler, not a settler, a true free spirit. You travel too, but you participate in your world. You identify life as an authentic journey, while Heath observed life, like he lost something, lost an intimacy he didn't recognize or never quite grasped. Can't explain it any better."

"Besides, I like younger men anyway."

She kisses the tip of his nose, the first truly affectionate contact between them.

"Yup, that's me. Tick, the younger. Fourteen minutes. We have different birthdays. Heath was born at eleven fifty-two I was born six minutes after midnight on February twenty-ninth. I've only had eight actual birthdays in my life. That's weird enough. We celebrated on the twenty-eighth, but for one day every leap year, Heath bragged he was a year older than me."

Silence stretches out. A minute pauses for eternity, then another. Emotion rolls in, wraps itself around two young bodies and inserts itself into two young minds. The wants and needs intensify and a long restrained obsession vibrates within two souls.

Ellie and Tick lock eyes, the physical desire eats them alive and for uncountable moments an impending release feeds upon that hunger as both acknowledge a truth.

"Touch me now, Tick, or we'll both explode. Been waiting too long."

Tick obeys her command, elicits a soft feminine squeak in response. The first magical kiss, tongues tangle and caress. Passion denied springs alive, embracing a man and a woman who finally abandon restraint, cross over that sensual and physical threshold together, engaging the exaltation and bliss that emotion drives in everything alive and conscious.

Ellie straddles his hips, staring down at her new lover, marveling once again at a mirror image reflecting its memory back at her. She moves with an age-old rhythm that comes as natural as breathing. Once again, the soft murmurs and passionate moans of a sexual union rise above the vagabond encampment, and bind two soul-mates for life.

A tear rolls down his cheek, then another. "I miss my brother."

Ellie wipes his eyes then her own. "Me too. Let's name the baby Teath."

His eyes pop wide open. "Really? A baby? Really?"

"Little over ten weeks, I even know the night. Not quite old enough to kick yet."

She takes his palm and lays it against her stomach. "A little Heath."

"Would've made him happy." Tick wraps his arms around Ellie, pulls her tight.

A streak of worry flits across his face. "Damn, we gotta get jobs."

Firelight flashes off a silver feather hanging off her left ear."Why spoil the fun?"

-30-

www.ingramcontent.com/pod-product-compliance
Lightning Source LLC
Chambersburg PA
CBHW030117180626
46812CB00002B/449